Passion and Glory

Book 2

Déception

Samantha Kaye

To Carol

Make the impossible
Possible.

ᴗ‿

Vince.

Casus Belli

"Principles without enforcement are like morals without restraint. Ignored by the strong and abused by the weak. And this is the current state of France."

The Chevalier de Chavanson nodded to acknowledge the pearl of shared wisdom uttered by his host, the Prince de Robervalle. Chavanson sat at one end of a long banquet table, staring in astonishment at the lavish extravagance of the banquet laid before him. He wore his finest court suit, tailored *à la disposition* with coat and waistcoat of wine-colored striped Lyons silk brocade, embroidered with sequin and mirror beads, and fabric wrapped buttons.[i] The ruffles of his sleeve and collar were needlepoint lace, and he sported a high crowned wig with enough powder to leave a conspicuous dusting on the shoulders of his jacket. Opposite him, at the other end of the long expanse of dining room table, which stretched to a length of more than twenty feet, sat the only other diner, his host, the Prince de Robervalle.

Chavanson felt part envy, part disgust at the enormous quantity of gold and silver everywhere on display and the purposeful superfluity of ten lackeys standing in attendance to serve a table of just two diners. He wondered how the prince could afford to live in such extravagance. The silver dish laid before him shone to such a mirror-like sheen, he could see his reflection with clarity in the plate, the long dueling scar which marred the left side of his face clearly visible under a thinly applied coat of powder and rouge. The scar had been gained in the aftermath of a successful duel and marked the only blemish to mar Chavanson's otherwise handsome face. He sported both the scar and his expensive suit with indifference. One earned as a badge of honor, the other worn as a mark of rank and position.

The chevalier sipped an excellent wine from a hand-made crystal goblet, crafted to standards suitable for a royal palace. While he drank, one of the valets began to fill his plate with selections from the more than sixty plates of prepared delicacies, while others showed off plates of the various foods on offer. Four soups, Spanish pates, rabbits on skewers, fowl wings a la marechale, larded breasts of mutton, sweetbreads en papillot, two spitted suckling pigs, fried turkey al la ravigote, loin of veal on a spit, all this and more for a working meal where the Prince wasn't even showing off. [ii]

As he admired the intricate design etched in lead on the goblet's stem, Chavanson considered how best to inform his wealthy, powerful and mercurial patron of the troubling news he had just received from the colonies.

"Monsieur le Prince, it seems your old nemesis has at last decided to come out of hiding. He's to marry off his eldest son to the daughter of a newly ennobled banker, a parvenu who styles himself Baron de Salvigny or something of the sort," Chavanson said, raising his voice so it would carry the length of the table to his host.

The prince put down his fork and looked up at his guest. He had a round face, with squirrel-like eyes shaded almost black, and a long straight nose. His heavily powdered visage produced the aspect of an animated marble bust, giving emphasis to a small mouth with rodent-like front teeth and very red lips. The condition of the prince's dentures was natural; the shade surrounding them was not. The prince liked red and applied the color in copious amounts to brighten his lips and cheeks. He had acquired the habit of overdoing things in his youth. It had begun as a small fault of character and evolved into a grotesque obsession with luxury, decadence and debauchery, which stood out even at Versailles, where love of excess had begun as fashion in the reign of Louis XIV and progressed to a disease under the current king. The prince wore a suit of red Lyon silk, with gold thread on the cuffs and lapels and engraved gold buttons to match. The polished gold buttons shone under the several hundred candles of the chandeliers like miniature setting suns. No king would have been shamed to wear the prince's garment, and it took a royal sized fortune to bear the cost of the cloth, tailoring and embroidery. An admirer of the English, the prince wore a wig in the buckle queue style known as the King George, with several added curls at the sides that evoked the days of his youth.[iii]

"*Bien bien bien bien voilà.* Blaise has allied Marbéville to a common nobody? I suspect the sized of the wench's dowry sufficiently covered his embarrassment at having to stoop so low to find a daughter-in-law. It seems the fortunes of his house have descended to new lows if circumstances have compelled him to barter his name for money. Not that such a thing saddens me. Quite the contrary. Our enemy's privation is always to our advantage and satisfaction. I suspect that the spectacle of an alliance based solely on ignoble practicality, should at last put an end to the rumors of his vaunted wealth. But I guess hobnobbing with common merchants and freeing his *Nègres* hasn't been as profitable as he had hoped."

The prince sat back with a smirk of satisfaction, pausing to take a deep tug from his cheroot of tobacco. He leaned to one side to watch the smoke dissipate as it rose toward the massive gilt chandelier above the table and its centuries of burning candles. As one lackey moved in to remove the thirteenth plate the prince had consumed during the meal and replace it with a fresh one, another approached to bring the prince more *Jerez*, as his master preferred the balancing taste of an Amontillado when he smoked, a habit acquired from the prince's time in England as a youth.

Chavanson waited until the lackeys withdrew before resuming the thread of conversation. "Perhaps not, but of more interest to Monsieur le Prince, might be the news that the marquis will move his family back to Paris, in preparation for his reinstatement at court. It appears he intends to try and retrieve his flagging fortunes by appealing to his friends there, of which there still remain quite a few who would support him."

Chavanson glanced up from his plate of roasted quail, anticipating the storm of the prince's reaction. It came quickly.

"*Non non non non non*! He would not dare such a thing!" the prince almost shouted. "The conditions of the understanding His Majesty forced upon us both were quite clear. Montferraud is to remain in the Colonies and away from Versailles. Anything else and I shall consider the terms of our agreement null and void. What makes you so certain he plans to return to France?"

Chavanson sucked the meat off the thigh of the excellent quail and spat the bone into his napkin. He placed the used napkin on the table and lackey number six instantly provided another in its place. "My information comes from an irrefutable source, Prince. I assure you it is accurate."

The prince threw his own napkin onto the table with disgust. "*Bien bien bien*. If this is so, then we must take measures to ensure we are well prepared to receive him and all his wretched kin in the manner they deserve. I should be glad to devise a special welcome for the mongrel *chienne*[iv] he married and her bastard. It's time we redeemed the debt of blood owed to our house in full."

Chavanson listened without emotion. It amused him that the prince sought to impugn the honor of Madame de

Blaise in such a vile manner, even though no one doubted the boy's parentage, only the specific composition of certain matrilineal bloodlines. Another indication of the depths of the prince's hatred for the marquis and by extension, all the Montferrauds. *How amusing to feed and twist his loathing to my own advantage.*

"I have taken the liberty of contacting the Baron de Ginestas, Prince. He has a talent for dealing with delicate problems, albeit for a price."

The prince waved away his lackeys, motioning for Chavanson to take the seat near him so they could speak in complete privacy. Once Chavanson had reseated himself closer to his host, the prince leaned in, gripping the chevalier with firmness on the arm.

"*Bien bien bien, mon bon ami.* We must tread with care in this matter. I can't afford to have anything traced back to me. My personal history with Blaise is a rare matter in which both politics and honor intertwine. If Ginestas is to be our tool he must be discreet *and* reliable," the prince cautioned.

Chavanson met his host's gaze with directness, convinced of the prudence of his choice. "He is both, Prince. You have but to command me and I will instruct him to arrange for a suitable message of warning to be sent to the Marquis de Blaise."

The prince returned his hands to his lap, fingering the silver signet on his right hand. "Prudence, prudence, prudence, young lion. Let us not use a cannon to frighten a mouse. Perhaps a warning shot across the bow will suffice to remind the marquis of our agreement and that I have neither forgotten, nor forgiven him for what he did to my family."

Chavanson nodded, despite his disappointment at the prince's reticence to act more boldly. "We are in full agreement, Prince. Neither of us wishes for the inconvenience of an inquiry, which the court might feel itself forced to make in the aftermath of any unpleasantness. However, I believe I have a suitable stratagem to make our point and yet keep the royal hounds of retribution at bay."

The prince waved a hand for the chevalier to continue, eager to hear the details of Chavanson's scheme.

"We shall leave Marbéville and Madame de Blaise untouched for now. To strike directly at them would be too obvious a move. Others might detect our hand and we have no wish to reveal our deeper strategy. We will strike instead at d'Argentolle. No one will act to support him, given who his mother is. His death will send a warning to the marquis not to be trifle with us, and it will provide a satisfying measure of blood vengeance as well. I shall arrange his ending in an untraceable manner, but it shall be bold enough so that the marquis will not mistake the message. If we adhere to my methods, we will also have the satisfaction of causing acute pain to Madame de Blaise. Pain your poor mother and daughter in-law were each forced to bear when their husbands were so brutally taken from them," Chavanson said, purposefully stoking the prince's resentment by reminding him of the full extent of his family's humiliation—a brother killed by the Marquis de Blaise in a duel, and his own son killed as well in attempting to reclaim the family's honor.

"I warned my brother not to be so rash with Blaise, but he would not listen. My son had the same hot temper as my brother and suffered for it," the prince said in excuse.

Chavanson decided not to point out that the prince's son had acted as the prince himself ought to have. He watched the prince take another sip of Amontillado, and wondered if the fine Jerez sufficed to wash away the traces of his cowardice.

"*Alors, alors, alors, alors*. You know what is at stake here. You're sure of the man's ability to accomplish such a delicate and difficult task?" the prince said.

"I am certain of it. D'Argentolle has something of a reputation as a duelist—a reputation built upon fighting nobodies and fops as a schoolboy. We shall lure him into an affair of honor his pride will not allow him to refuse—one which seems a trifle on the surface, but whose real dangers lie well-submerged, concealed by a subtlety unfathomable to one of such shallow understanding. Whatever the result, he will not survive the contest. An obscure and deadly poison upon the blade will see to his certain and untraceable demise," Chavanson explained with a triumphant grin.

The prince smiled with measured cruelty, well pleased his young protégé displayed all the cunning and ruthlessness needed to advance in the one game which obsessed them both—the great lust for power. "*Bien, bien, bien, eh bien!* Make it so, and inform me when you have succeeded. I shall not forget this service, my dear chevalier. You shall see that I know how to reward my friends and punish my enemies."

Chavanson inclined his head in a respectful bow. "Your friendship is the only reward I seek, Monsieur le Prince. I shall begin matters at once. Leave everything to me. The warning to the Marquis de Blaise will be delivered soon. Whether he heeds it or not, d'Argentolle's life shall be forfeit. By my word and your consent, he henceforth bears the mark of the Black Fleur-de-lis—a mark of death from which he cannot escape."

*

The Baron de Salvagnac waved away the servant who approached to fill his glass of claret. He glanced down the length of the long table at his family, all gathered around him for the evening meal. The mood of the *souper* was tense and uncomfortable, far from the usual relaxed and pleasant atmosphere he prized after a long day spent with his clerks and figures. A sullenness of disposition existed between his wife and eldest daughter, which disturbed him. Moreover, the relationship with the Montferrauds, which had begun so well, seemed to have hit a very rough patch, and he could not fathom why.

"I tell you, my dear; it's all quite curious and vexing. For reasons I have yet to discover, an impasse now exists between us, though I can't fathom why or even when it developed," the baron said.

Madame de Salvagnac listened to her husband with only half an ear. She gazed about the dining room table, infuriated that her niece had chosen to skip another meal. *Does she think her pretenses will break my resolve? I will not let such willful and ill-tempered conduct dissuade me. She must learn that obedience is the sacrosanct duty of every woman. It is a reality she must learn to accept, lest she become a disgrace to us all.*

The baronne set down her silver soupspoon and turned to address the steward. "Have the vicomtesse sent for at once. I grow tired of her absences and feigned illness. She must come down and join the rest of her family, even if you have to carry her down!"

The steward nodded toward one of the maids in attendance, who set off immediately to fetch the vicomtesse. Julienne's brow furrowed with concern as she watched the girl depart. Madame de Salvagnac, however, returned her attentions to her husband and her soup.

"What is it precisely you speak of, my dear friend?" the baronne asked.

"Why, the marriage arrangements, of course. My lawyers tell me the papers finalizing the marriage contract have all been prepared for some time now and require only the marquis' signature to complete, yet he still delays in signing them. I have tried on more than one occasion to determine the reasons for his reluctance, but he has so far refused to provide a satisfactory reply, either through his letters or to me directly, I tell you."

"Perhaps he's simply been too busy with other affairs," the baronne suggested.

"I also believed he might wish to take refuge behind such a pretext, Madame, which is why I even went so far as to call on him unannounced at his estate. I had hoped to confront him at his residence in the belief that a more direct approach might allow us to settle any outstanding matters between us. I arrived unannounced only to be told he was away, despite all his carriages being in plain view in the courtyard. I regret to say it, but I'm afraid I'm beginning to wonder if he's having second thoughts about the marriage *and* the alliance."

Julienne raised her head from her plate, eyes darting from her mother to her father with alarm. Though everyone's demeanor at table appeared outwardly calm, underneath the tranquil façades, conflicts and emotions roiled with unseen turbulence. Madame de Salvagnac finished her delicious bowl of leek and turtle soup. She waited for the place setting to be cleared before she spoke.

"Such behavior does seem out of character for the marquis. Do you feel with certainty matters have deteriorated to such an extent? Surely, nothing has occurred which another visit cannot cure. Perhaps we might invite Monsieur de Blaise and Monsieur de Marbéville to dine with us this week. I'll have the cooks prepare a special feast in their honor," the baronne suggested with eagerness.

The baron shook his head. "I have already made such inquiries on my own, and sent several invitations. I have received nothing from father or son but excuses. It is possible the marquis found a better match and now wants to break things off with us. With the old aristocracy, one never knows what to think. At least we have the public announcement with which to hold him to his honor and to extract perhaps our pound of flesh. It is all very strange though. Before I left for Martinique to attend to my affairs there, things seemed to be in an excellent state. The suddenness of this breach is just so damned peculiar."

The coarseness of her husband's language startled the baronne. He did not normally resort to the use of common vulgarities in his speech, even under extreme duress. Her daughters noticed as well, but they too seemed inclined to ignore it.

The baron looked at Julienne, his expression both curious and dour, as if perhaps she might be able to shed more light on the reasons behind the sudden coldness of the marquis and his eldest son. "Julienne, my dear. In the time you spent at the marquis' estate, did you receive any warning at all of an impending breach?"

Julienne glanced at her mother before replying. "No, Papa. Our relations with everyone were quite cordial and warm. In his letters to me, Francis has always expressed only the most tender and sincere consideration."

The baron rubbed his chin. He seemed to take little solace from this response. "It's been more than two weeks since your departure. Have you received any communication from the comte since then?"

Julienne looked accusingly at her mother, a glance that did not escape the baron's notice. "No, Papa."

"And you are of course still…that is…all is still intact?"

Julienne blushed with indignation. "Of course, Papa!"

The baron shook his head in perplexity. "Well then, well then. I wonder what could have happened to bring about such an abrupt change. It is very peculiar. Very peculiar I tell you."

A small commotion drew everyone's attention. Sérolène entered the room in response to her aunt's summons, assisted by a pair of maids. She seemed as pale as a ghost, and projected a pitiable air of weakness and frailty. The baron watched with concern as the maids led the vicomtesse to a chair and helped her to sit. Her eyes seemed dull and lifeless, drifting in the hollow of an expressionless face, and she appeared to be suffering from a fever of unknown severity. All eyes looked upon her with sympathy save those of her aunt, which shone cold and indifferent.

The baron's worried gaze reflected his concern. "What ails you, my dear niece? You do not look at all well. Goodness me, how long has she been in such a state?"

Julienne answered for her *cousine*, casting another sharp glance toward her mother. "She has been this way ever since we returned from the marquis' estate, Papa."

The baron glanced accusingly at his wife. "Why have the doctors not been sent for in my absence? We must call for them at once, just to be sure. I've heard there have been several reported cases of a serious fever in the Cap."

The baron gazed at Sérolène with sympathetic concern. "Can you perhaps take some nourishment, my dear child?"

Sérolène sat listless and unmoving in her chair. "I don't know, Uncle. I'm not at all hungry."

Madame de Salvagnac appeared unmoved. "Of course she can. Bring her some soup at once. If she's unable to get it down, you may open her mouth and spoon it in for her."

The baron bristled at the harshness of his wife's tone. A servant placed a bowl of soup before Sérolène, who stared at the creamy green liquid with dull and vacant eyes.

"My dear, do you think such a stern approach is *utile,* given her obvious frailty?" the baron said.

Madame de Salvagnac placed her napkin on the table. She covered it with her hand and slowly curled it into a fist. "Some weaknesses must be treated with more diligence than others to prevent an even more serious affliction. There is your soup, Mademoiselle. It is quite delicious. Eat up, and no excuses!"

Sérolène turned to look at her aunt with a vacant stare, as if she had already lost the simple thread of her aunt's instruction. She seemed to struggle with even the rudimentary task of taking hold of her spoon, but with an effort, lifted the jittering silver ladle to her lips. She took spoonful after spoonful, swallowing each with apparent difficulty. It took several minutes, but she managed at last to get most of the liquid down as the rest of the family watched in cautious, uneasy silence.

The baronne regarded the nearly empty bowl, her eyes animated with satisfaction at the victory claimed over her niece's recalcitrance. "You see what can be achieved when one is resolved not to be dissuaded?"

Julienne, however, continued to watch her *cousine* with concern, noting the faraway look in Sérolène's eyes. "Lena? Lena!"

Sérolène slumped to the side, collapsing against the chair to her left. As her head struck the back of the empty seat, the contents of her stomach spewed out with force, soiling her dress and spilling onto the white tablecloth, the regurgitated soup mixed in patches with blood. Éléonore screamed and covered her eyes. Sérolène slid to the floor in a crumpled heap, throwing the entire household into chaos.

"Please, won't someone help her?" Julienne pleaded.

The baron shot to his feet. "Carry my niece to her room and send for the doctor at once!" he shouted.

Two lackeys lifted Sérolène and carried her away as Éléonore's cries of grief rang through the dining room, a portent of the bitter trials yet to come.

*

Julienne sat close by her mother in the *salon de compagnie,* waiting for the doctor to complete his examination of the vicomtesse. Both mother and daughter remained separated by a wide poisonous gulf of reproach, a part of the general unease which had spread through the house after the disaster of the meal, like smoke from a clogged hearth. No one seemed able to lift the pall.

"I'm sure she'll be fine. It's just nerves and the fact she hasn't been eating well," the baronne said. Her words seemed directed as much to herself, as they were to her daughter.

Julienne shook her head. "I very much hope so, Maman, but if she does recover, it'll be no thanks to your efforts."

"I've done only my duty. No more, no less," the baronne protested. "And if my niece had the sense and the character to have done hers as well, this might all have been avoided. Surely you can't think to blame *me* for what's occurred."

Julienne appeared exasperated at the cold, aloof nature of her mother's words and the unwillingness to accept any responsibility for provoking Sérolène's collapse. "Then who are we to blame, Maman? Nicolas? Or better yet, poor Madame de Blaise, whom you seem to believe is the fount of all ills? Of course, it's much more convenient to lay fault at the Montferrauds' door than to admit your part in the disaster your own mischief and neglect have wrought."

The baronne had grown accustomed to having her way with her husband and children and bristled that Julienne would have the nerve to contest with her in so defiant a manner. "You forget yourself, Mademoiselle. I know this little episode has upset you and you are not yourself, else I would take great issue with your words and the insolence of your tone."

Julienne glared at her mother. "You are right, Maman. I am not myself, nor should I wish to be when my sweet *cousine*, who has never done harm to anyone, lies so stricken in her bed that her life may be at risk, and it is we who have placed her there, we who have stood by and watched and said nothing as her spirit ebbed away before our eyes. Did you think your sternness the answer for her broken heart? Did I not caution you that if something did not occur to break the cycle of her melancholy, she might slip so far into misery that we would be unable to recover her? Would you prefer, Maman that she die rather than be with the one she loves, who loves her with equal ardor and sincerity?"

The baronne glared back with equal defiance. "How can you accuse me of such vile desires? Her blood is my blood. I could never wish for such a thing. I want only what is best for her in the long run. We do not know that her condition is as bleak as you claim, or that such matters as you allude to are at the root of it. More likely it's just a temporary illness, a result of the food."

Julienne broke down in tears. "Oh, Maman, can we not at least be honest with each other? Let us not pretend we do not know she is dying, and her broken heart is the cause of it."

The baronne opened her mouth to justify her actions once more to Julienne, but the return of her husband in the company of the doctor preempted any further defense. The baron's face appeared drawn and fraught with concern, and the demeanor of the physician did nothing to lift any hopes. The doctor whispered something at length to the baron before turning to address the entire room.

"The vicomtesse has a very high fever which we are unable to break. If it continues for more than twenty-four hours, it is doubtful there will be anything we can do to save her," the doctor explained.

Julienne gasped and rushed into her father's arms, unable to hold back tears, which streamed freely down her cheeks. Visibly affected by the seriousness of the prognosis,

17

the baronne averted her eyes form Julienne, who shot her mother a pleading look. Madame de Salvagnac remained with her head bowed, listening in stoic silence.

The doctor searched each face in the room. "Her heart and pulse are very weak. The cause is uncertain, but I believe it to be one of acute tension and nervous stress, compounded by her failure to eat. I regret to say it, but we often see similar signs in young girls who have experienced some very tragic disappointment. I understand she had been recuperating from a fall suffered some weeks ago. It is common to see a relapse several weeks after a blow to the head. In this case, I feel such circumstances are only contributory matters to her current condition. I cannot say what is at the root of what ails her. I only know it is not a common or known fever we are dealing with, but some deeper and heavy malaise. Her greatest hope now is her own resolve. Each one of you must do all you can to strengthen it. If she has no desire to get better, no will to live, there is little I can do. I am sure the care and affection of her family will help in bolstering her determination, but you will know with certainty within a day—two at most—how to prepare yourselves. The persistence of the fever will be your guide."

The doctor paused again to look from face to face. "I shall return tomorrow to examine the vicomtesse again. In the meantime, I have given her something to help her rest for the moment, and perhaps recover some of her strength. I do not wish to rob you of all hope, but I caution you, in her weakened condition, she has but two chances in ten of surviving."

Having said and done all he could, the doctor bowed his regrets, leaving each of the Salvagnacs to their own thoughts and fears. The baron stood with an arm around Julienne to console her, a faraway look in his eyes. The pain on his face plain for all to see. He struggled to hold back his emotions. "I am at a complete loss as to how this all occurred so suddenly. Only a few weeks ago she had never appeared happier or more carefree. What could have happened since her return to drive her emotions to such an extreme and bring on this troubled and now potentially fatal state?"

Julienne still clung to her father, unable to accept the doctor's bleak prognosis. She looked at her mother to answer, but the baronne only looked down at her hands. *Enough! I can no longer play a part in this. Have there ever been greater miscalculations than those Maman has made, first with Madame de Blaise, and now with poor Lena? If she should die, have they any idea how Nicolas and his family will react? Now I understand what Francis asked of me. I must choose—either the misguided scruples of my family, or what is right. If I do not, then all our hopes will turn to ashes.*

Julienne turned toward her father, a resolute set to her jaw. "I know how to save her, Papa, but if we are to have any hope, you must have faith in me and you must act at once."

The baron looked at his daughter in astonishment. "What? The doctor professed himself at a loss as to what to do. How can you possibly..."

"You must send your fastest horseman for the Chevalier d'Argentolle, Papa. Only he is capable of saving her now."

"What? The chevalier?"

"There's no time now to explain. If you wish to save my *cousine's* life, then do as I beg you and summon him here at once!" Julienne pleaded.

19

The baron stared at his daughter, then at his wife. Madame de Salvagnac nodded in agreement. "Do as she counsels, husband. I fear it is our best, if not our only hope."

Stunned into silence, the baron rang for his steward, who appeared within moments of the summons. "Fetch my groom and ready the fastest horse to take a message to the Chevalier d'Argentolle. Julienne, as you seem to know the cause of her distress, perhaps you can write to the chevalier and best explain to him the seriousness of the situation. As soon as you have completed the letter, we shall have it delivered. I need not remind you the importance of saving every moment."

Julienne's face glowed with gratitude. "At once, Papa."

The baron placed a hand on Julienne's arm to delay her. "Before you begin your letter, I wish to know if his actions are the root cause of what disturbs her."

"Not *his* actions, Papa, but ours. We are the ones who have so injured her."

"That is neither just nor correct," the baronne interjected.

"It is both, Maman, and I fear, the cause of our greater misfortune as well, Papa. Did Maman neglect to inform you of the many cultivated slights and insults she made toward Madame de Blaise, or of the disgraceful manner of our flight from the marquis' estate?" Julienne said, her words a vengeful but fair repayment for the blows she had received in the carriage.

The baron looked from his wife to his daughter in astonishment. Julienne, who out of concern for Sérolène, had withheld her true feelings since their return from the marquis' estate, now realized the time had come for her to speak with frankness.

"You've wished for some time to know the cause of the breach between our families. How else, Papa, would you expect the marquis to behave toward us, when we have behaved in so disgraceful a manner ourselves? Need I remind everyone his son nearly died in rescuing Lena and my sister? Yet while the rest of the world acclaims the chevalier for his valor, we, it seems, who are soon to be his family, are content to insult the boy's mother and keep company and counsel with her slanderers. In the wake of such reprehensible conduct, I should think it a wonder, Papa, if Monsieur le Marquis de Blaise should desire to treat with us at all, let alone ally his family to ours."

Madame de Salvagnac stabbed a finger of accusation at her daughter. "Ungrateful child! How dare you speak in such an insolent manner and tone?"

"Why am I to be deemed ungrateful, Madame? Because I refuse to let your misguided scruples destroy my happiness or the fortunes of our entire family?" Julienne shouted back.

Confounded by her daughter's defiance, a dumbfounded Madame de Salvagnac turned to her husband to seek his intervention. "Monsieur de Salvagnac. Will you allow your child to speak to me in so reprehensible a manner?"

The baron raised his hands for silence. "My dear Julienne, go write your letter, and then return here to me as soon as it is done."

Julienne accepted her father's intervention without question. "Yes, Papa. I shall return as quickly as I can."

21

"See that you do, my child. For your poor *cousine's* sake. This night, time is a thing we cannot afford to waist."

*

The baron paced the length of the sitting room, his eyes cast down on the polished mahogany floor. The light of the sitting room's candles danced upon the gleaming wood. He stopped his pacing and turned his full attention toward his wife. "Now, Madame, as I am still in the dark as to the principal circumstances of this whole affair, would you please enlighten me as to the particulars of what you and my eldest daughter appear to be contesting?"

The baronne crossed the room to sit on the loveseat, which by coincidence happened to be her niece's favorite. Clasping her hands together in her lap, she turned toward the baron and began to explain. "After the incident at the Cap..."

"You mean the incident in which the Chevalier d'Argentolle saved the lives of our niece, our daughter, Mademoiselle de Vaudreuil and her governess?" the baron interrupted.

"Yes," Madame de Salvagnac replied, but the manner of her response made it clear she considered Nicolas' bravery to be of the most trivial sort.

"As I said, after the incident in the Cap, I sent our daughter to the marquis' estate to be a responsible chaperone for our niece as she convalesced, and to look after the larger family interests."

"And you feel our daughter did not accomplish this to your satisfaction?"

"How can I feel otherwise, when she allowed the establishment of an illicit liaison between Sérolène and that *Nègre* boy! I have the proof of it in a letter from Madame Dupluie. That is what prompted my behavior on the day I went to collect them. Please tell me what wrong I did in acting as I have."

Before the baron could answer, Julienne returned with the letter intended for Nicolas, delivering it into her father's hands. He read it, nodded his satisfaction, and then sealed it with his mark. Before the wax had cooled to paper, the steward returned to announce the arrival of the fast horse the baron had requested. The baron handed his steward the letter.

"Give this to the courier and tell him he is to deliver it himself into the chevalier's own hands. Tell him to ride the beast to death if he must, but I want the chevalier here before sunrise!"

"Yes, Monseigneur!" the steward replied, bowing as he hurried out with the letter.

The baron then returned his attention to Julienne. "Your mother tells me your *cousine* has fallen in love with the Chevalier d'Argentolle. Is this true?"

Julienne seemed neither surprised nor cowed by the question. "Yes, Papa."

"And he professes to love her as well?" the baron continued.

"Yes, Papa, and very dearly."

"I see. And this is how he shows his affection, by breaking her heart?"

"He did not injure her, Papa. Maman forbade Lena to see him again. That is the reason she suffers so," Julienne explained.

The baron looked over at his wife, who remained defiantly silent, thus confirming the truth of Julienne's words. He returned his gaze to his daughter. "And so your solution to the problem is to allow such an impossible and unsuitable liaison to continue?"

Julienne gaze remained as firm and unyielding as her father's. "Impossible, Papa? Why must it be so? You did not deem him so unsuitable when his heroism saved Lena, Charlotte, and Éléonore. Did you not come to visit him yourself and pay your respects? Unless circumstances have suddenly changed, is he not also a vicomte of France and a chevalier in his own right? Why should their feelings for each other be impossible?"

"Titles are not the only measure of a man. Besides, can he speak of any fortune? As second son he'll inherit nothing but lavish tastes he can't afford," the baronne interjected.

"I quite agree with you on the first part, Maman. Titles are not the only measure of worth. The chevalier has already proven his value by deed, has he not? As for the second point, Francis himself told me Nicolas possesses an annual income of more than a quarter of a million livres a year.[v] I should have presumed *such a person* a very agreeable proposition for most young ladies of quality. What's more, he adores Lena as much as she adores him."

Julienne watched her mother. The baronne seemed shocked by the enormity of the sum and did not try to mask her astonishment. Her father's surprise lasted but a moment.

"But we are not most, my girl, and his mother is a Negress. Are you aware of what that means, you little fool?" the baronne said.

"I am aware, Maman, that His Majesty himself approved the marriage of Monsieur and Madame de Blaise, as well as her assumption of the rank of marquise. If our sovereign saw fit to elevate and confirm her to such high station, pray tell me, who are we to judge her ill?"

The back and forth exchange between his wife and daughter did little to improve the baron's mood or alter his opinion. Though he tried to consider Julienne's arguments with objectivity, he seemed unconvinced he should agree to consider the Chevalier d'Argentolle as a potential suitor for his niece, grand fortune or not. Some things money could *not* buy. He of all people knew this better than most.

"My dear daughter, it will mean a great deal to general society and to those at court. Have you any idea what will be said about your *cousine* or about all of us if she were to be matched with the chevalier?"

"Matched?" the baronne interrupted in protest. "Husband, how can you even say such a thing? Surely you cannot agree to ruin us by allowing a brutish black whelp to..."

"Silence, Madame! I believe you have said and done quite enough for one day!" the baron said with exasperation.

Madame de Salvagnac recoiled in shock, appalled at the unaccustomed display of temper from her husband. She hung her head in obedient silence, too surprised and cowed to reply.

Julienne turned a pleading gaze toward her father. "I think the prospect of a life full of his love, would make whatever censure she might receive more than bearable, Papa. A broken heart cannot sustain itself on the tasteless morsels dropped from the table of strangers. Nor will it take nourishment from professions of esteem from those who are of no relation or concern to any of us. She may seem just a girl to you, Papa, but I know her heart is a woman's heart. It loves and yearns, and aches. And if not tended with care, it can also break."

The baron began to pace the floor as he considered his reply. "I just don't know, my dear. I believe myself to be a prudent and a fair man, but this…this asks very much indeed."

"There is also the small matter of my own fate," Julienne reminded her father. "Such considerations must, of course, take the smaller part when Lena lies so gravely ill, but in the time I have spent amongst the Montferrauds, I have come to know them well, Papa. Francis has on more than one occasion told me of his love and respect for Madame de Blaise, and I need not point out to anyone how devoted he and Nicolas are to each other. They are a proud family, Papa, and a very close one. If we are to unite with them, then it shall be all or nothing. You cannot drive a wedge between them based on Maman's scruples or lack of them, nor seek to gain advantage from one brother at the expense of the other. Neither honor nor their regard for each other will allow it to be done."

The baron looked up, his brows furrowed together in worry. For the first time, he appeared quite old and frail. Julienne seemed to realize then the heavy burden he had to carry for them all. She put her arms around his neck. Her lips caressed his cheek in tender devotion. "You are among the best of men, Papa, and I love you dearly. Decide as you must,

26

but I tell you this with complete sincerity. I have met no man gentler or more honest than the Comte de Marbéville. I have met no nobler or more honorable man than the Chevalier d'Argentolle. Perhaps the grand Madame Dupluie keeps to better society amongst the infallible ducs and princes, but we mortals must make do with more practical fare. I know you have always loved us and wished the best for us, Papa. This is why I now most humbly beg you not to break two hearts for a cause which will profit you neither in honor, nor riches, nor esteem."

Julienne turned with reluctance toward her mother, embracing her as well to complete her self-imposed penitence for having dared to offer her opinions with such unbridled passion. "Forgive me, dear parents, if my words have seemed intemperate. Perhaps they were so, but they were truly heartfelt. Please excuse me. I shall leave you to decide as you must and go to render what comfort I can to my dear *cousine*."

Julienne slipped quietly from the room, leaving her parents together in their lingering unease. Madame de Salvagnac cast her eyes toward her husband, still unsure of the baron's current state of humor. "What are we to do now, husband?"

The baron let out a heavy sigh. "I fear Julienne may be right. We may have no other choice but to let things proceed as they may."

The baronne stared at her husband in surprise. "But he's a *Nègre*!"

"His mother may or may not be part African. Does this make him a *Nègre*, just because you and your crowd of salon gossips and White Hatters are so fond of repeating the slander?" the baron challenged. "In preparation for our

27

daughter's marriage, I and my lawyers have also done some checking into the origins of Madame de Blaise and the Montferrauds in general. Her father's patent of nobility from the court of Norway dates back over five hundred years, and as for the Marquis de Blaise, of course I need not remind you how blue his blood is—*Chevalier d'épée, grand, haut et puissant seigneur*; comtés of Marbéville, Vignori, Argentolle, and Blécourt, not to mention the marquisate of Blaise with an income reported to be worth well over a million livres a year! It is the reason you were so eager for an alliance in the first place, is it not. And the boy, whatever the particular composition or chemistry of his blood, is also by law and custom, chevalier, vicomte, and a *gentilhomme de nom et d'armes,*[vi] with all the rights and privileges those respective ranks and titles entail, I tell you."

The baron lifted his head expecting his wife to protest or attempt to repudiate his assertions, but she chose instead to remain silent. "Nothing to say? No refutations to cite from your penurious Gallic informant? Good, for I have some other *nouvels* which might interest you concerning the chevalier. The École Militaire accepted him two years early on the signature of no less than the Prince de Montbarrey himself! What does *this* suggest to you as far as his merit is concerned?"

The baronne's questioning gaze reflected her surprise. "But how can that be true? It is the most prestigious military school in all of France, perhaps all of Europe. Several of my friends, even those well connected at court have been unable to procure places there for their sons. You're sure this is true?"

"Oh yes, Madame. I still have my sources, though I would wager even money the marquis himself does not yet know that Montbarrey has approved the application. They say the boy's marks were so high at Brienne his teachers did not know what more to do with him. They even refused to publish the final list of prizes given out by the Comte de Brienne last year because *he won them all,* in *every* subject, I tell you! The Brothers feared accusations of cheating, so they suppressed the true results. And the boy's penchant for dueling apparently gave them serious pause.

"Dueling? But he's far too young to take part in such affairs," Madame de Salvagnac scoffed.

"Be that as it may, Madame, I have it on good authority he fought several duels in his last year at school—more than a dozen in all since he arrived, the first at age nine! It's one of the reasons they sought to have him complete his studies early."

The baronne leapt at once on the revelation of such a flaw. "But such actions hardly speak favorably of his character. What could he have to fight over at such an age?"

"I understand in almost all the cases mentioned he fought in defense of his mother's honor, Madame. Given this reason and his youth, the authorities were inclined to overlook his indiscretions."

"Did none of those he encountered deign to make an accusatory report?"

"I don't think anyone would wish it to be known they have been beaten in an affair of honor by a schoolboy. The reports say the chevalier is something of a magician with the blade. You saw his physique for yourself. By any measure he looks a young Hercules," the baron said.

The baronne looked at her husband as if to respond, but at length decided to remain silent.

"We must open our eyes to the reality of the times, Madame. Let us not allow antiquated opinions and prejudices to drag us down. The chevalier saved the lives of our daughter, niece, and others at considerable risk to himself. Is your heart so uncharitable as to have forgotten the cost of his valor? Do you think the Vaudreuils have overlooked what he did for Charlotte and her governess? For if you do, you should know Amiral Vaudreuil's personal intervention is a principal cause for the recent astounding social resurrection of Madame de Blaise."

"Monsieur de Vaudreuil? But was always one of the staunchest supporters of the exclusionary policy," the baronne pointed out.

"More proof, Madame, as to just how much things have changed. I presume it has also not escaped your notice that the marquise has also become the darling of the salons. Why, even your favorite, the Comtesse de Talonge, now considers her an intimate. If you think her opinions unimportant, go then and ask our Governor the Comte d'Argout, what he thinks now of the boy and his mother. I'd wager the old letch might even be content to have the chevalier as a son-in-law himself—that's how popular he is now, I tell you. Of course, if the staggering amount of the chevalier's yearly income became known to our peers, I'm sure your friends among his detractors would trample us to death in the rush to ally their own daughters to him."

The baron began to pace the room in earnest, the movement of his feet lubricating the fluidity of his thoughts. "Besides, with his pedigree and fortune, Sérolène would be better off with him as a husband, if he really loves her, than with some old comte who'd abandon her for his lover as soon as the dowry was in his hands."

"Then you mean to let them…"

30

The baronne's words trailed off, her tongue unable to form the words that described a circumstance she so abhorred and opposed.

"I'm not quite sure what I intend to do at this point. What I will not do is act with rashness. There are many things at stake here, some of which you do not know about— a legacy from the last Vicomte de La Bouhaire, for one."

Madame de Salvagnac raised her head with interest. "What do you mean, Monsieur? I had understood the terms of my late brother's will were straightforward."

"Not in the least, Madame. Your brother, you see, remained most concerned about the future welfare of his only child, both in terms of the financial security she should have, and about the power of choice he desired granted over her eventual state of marriage. To this end, he left a substantial dowry and a separate fortune to her, to ensure she would be a most welcome catch when she came of age. I know this must come as a surprise to you. You probably were left to believe that your father squandered all of your family's fortune.

Agnès nodded. "Yes. That is what we always believed. And the penury of our upbringing cemented the proof. How much did my brother leave her?"

"I am not at liberty, Madame, to divulge the exact amount, but it quite dwarfs what we shall provide for Julienne, and you are well aware of how excessive we are to be in that regard."

Madame de Salvagnac started to say something stopped herself. She stared at her husband, waiting for him to continue.

"What you must also know, Madame, is that the dowry left to our niece is less than a tenth of the direct fortune she is to receive as the sole heir to the principal part of your late brother's lands, estates, titles, and etcetera. The reputed fortune of your mother is no myth, Madame, but your brother hid it so well that not even the covetous eyes of the court could discover it. He knew that until she came of age, she and her fortune would be a target of the rapacious villains at court. And so he made it appear as if she had nothing to protect her. Our niece is rich beyond Croesus—at least she will be when she turns seventeen, when she is to receive the first part of her birthright. The full inheritance comes into effect only when she marries, and that event must also await her seventeenth birthday."

The baronne grasped the sides of her chair, her knuckles white with the force of her grip. "We always believed Maman's lost treasure to be just a fairy tale. However, it is real, you say? How astounding! And the stipulations of the legacy, they're all enforceable?"

"Oh yes, my dear, I've had the best lawyers looking into it for years. Your brother was quite thorough and added many secret protocols to his will. Much of his wealth he hid abroad in foreign banks, out of the reach of the court. In addition to the estates, which he entailed upon me at his death, the contract stipulated we raise Sérolène as one of our own. I also received a substantial amount in cash, to ensure her proper care. The estate will pay us a sum equal to what I received upon his death, when she marries. So you see we stand to gain in a substantial manner from allowing our niece to follow her heart, provided it meets the terms of the will," the baron explained.

The baron gestured toward the many gilt objects all around the room, and the expensive drapes, tapestries, and ornate furniture. "If our niece dies before she marries, for

32

whatever reason, both the future bequest is forfeit, and worse, half of the original cash grant must be returned within one month to the executor. I assure you, Madame, this is a sum which your love for copious and conspicuous *objets* and decorations, has long since removed from our coffers."

The baronne put her hand to her mouth in horror. "If she had been killed in town by that runaway team?"

"If the chevalier had not been willing to throw his life away in order to save our niece, then rich as I am—and I am very rich—I would likely be languishing now in the much less comfortable surroundings of debtor's prison, and you, Madame, in the Salpêtrière,[viii]" the baron said grimly.

"Bankrupt!" The baronne exclaimed, whispering the word as the curse it was.

"Yes, bankrupt, but for the bravery of the young man you are so happy to denigrate. It is not that we are so very poor, Madame, but we are rather stretched at the moment. Speculations have not been favorable to us of late, and the expenses to secure the marriage of Julienne have been large and predominantly in cash. A hint that I might be vulnerable could prove the single ember needed to ignite the conflagration of a run on my bank. We must avoid such an event and the harm it would do us at all costs. Now perhaps you see why I take an altogether different view of this so-called liaison than in other circumstances might be warranted, and why I will do all I can to ensure that our niece recovers her strength and her health."

"Dear God, Monsieur, how right you were to send for the chevalier! Do you think he will come? And if he does, is there still time?" the baronne asked, forced by circumstances to at last acknowledge the debt of gratitude they owed to

33

Nicolas, and the corresponding enormity of her mistake in offending Madame de Blaise.

The baron's expression deepened. "It's in God's hands now, Madame. We can only pray the chevalier has a forgiving heart, and a very swift horse."

*

"Monseigneur, an urgent letter has come for you!"

Nicolas squinted against the flickering candlelight as his valet approached his bedside. "All right, Julius, bring it to me. By God, what time is it?"

"Just past one in the morning, Monseigneur. Here is the letter. The man who brought it came from Monsieur de Salvagnac and insisted on delivering it himself. I promised to give it to you right away. He's ridden a fine horse to death to bring it, so I imagined it must be important," Julius said with urgency.

Nicolas read the seal and tore open the letter. As his eyes raced along the page, his blood froze in his veins. "Saddle my horse at once. The vicomtesse is taken ill, and I must go to her side. Wake my brother and show him this letter. He will know what to do. Go now! I will dress myself. In no more than ten minutes I must be on my way!"

Julius hurried from the room to carry out his orders. Nicolas rushed to don stockings, breeches, boots, riding coat, hat, gloves, and sword. Once dressed, he hastened through the darkened hallways of the estate on his way to the stables. He encountered his brother Francis as he reached the main vestibule.

The comte rushed toward Nicolas, still in his dressing gown and cap. He grasped Nicolas by the shoulders. "Dear God, Nicolas, I just read Julienne's letter! I came at once to find you."

"I must be off, Francis. You see from the urgency of the letter that they fear the worst. I must go and be with her."

"Of course. I will explain everything. I'll send some men to follow you as escort and as surety in case of injury to your horse. Go now, brother, go and may God be with you and your vicomtesse!"

Nicolas embraced his brother and then ran off toward the stables. When he arrived, he found Julius already there, holding the reins of Gigiana. The mare stood saddled and ready.

"Follow after me as swiftly as you can, Julius, I dare not tarry even a moment longer,"

Nicolas mounted up and put spurs to the flanks of his favorite mount. For the first time since he had ridden her, she felt the whip to her flanks as well. "Fly, my girl, fly like the wind! For tonight we race against death itself!"

*

The baron entered quietly into Sérolène's *chambre*. The cloying sweet-sick odor of medicines and perspiration hung in the air like a cloud of impending doom. Several lamps lit the room, illuminating the pallid face of the patient lying on the bed.

"Has there been any noticeable change?" the Baron de Salvagnac asked.

Julienne shook her head, her face furrowed with anxiety and concern. "I fear she slips further and further away from us, Papa. On occasion, she calls out in confusion. Once she even opened her eyes and appeared to recognize me, but the fever continues unabated."

"It seems we have acted too late. You look exhausted. Will you not come away and rest? I fear you've done all you can do for her," the baron said somberly.

Julienne noted the greying light of approaching dawn outside the drawn curtains. "I'm fine, Papa. Please let me stay. I do not wish to abandon her now. Has there been no word from Nicolas?"

The baron shook his head, his eyes full of disappointment. "Perhaps in light of the circumstances of your departure, he feels enough wronged not to respond to your plea."

Julienne sighed, she seemed greatly distressed to think her father might be right. She took a cool, damp cloth from the basin of water beside the bed, then bathed Sérolène's forehead with the moistened towel in an effort to ease her *cousine's* suffering.

"Julie…is that you?" Sérolène said.

The voice sounded very faint. Julienne motioned the baron closer to her *cousine's* sickbed. "Yes, it's me dear Lena. I'm here with Papa,"

"Water…if you please…" Sérolène said weakly.

Julienne reached for the pitcher on the table near the bed and poured her *cousine* a glass, supporting Sérolène's head as she helped her to drink. "You must try to get better, Lena, we're all so worried for you."

"Yes, my dear niece, we have all been very much concerned."

A long pause ensued before Sérolène responded. "It's best to let me go now, I beg you. I don't wish to be a burden to anyone anymore."

"You must not think that way, Lena. There are so many who love you, who need you. Think of your family. Think of me," Julienne pleaded, her voice breaking with sadness.

The baron lifted his head. The sound of a horse, arriving at the triple gallop echoed in the distance. "Do you hear that?"

Julienne nodded her head. They both heard an exhausted whinnying, followed by a loud thump. The baron's face lightened with optimism. "Perhaps he is here! I shall return presently. You must stay with her and give her hope."

The baron hurried out of the room. Julienne grasped Sérolène's hand. It felt hot to the touch. Sérolène closed her eyes. "No more doctors, Julie. Please. I feel so empty inside...perhaps death will bring me peace at last."

Julienne pressed her lips to Sérolène's hand, her tears leaving streaks of water along the lines of her *cousine's* palm. "Please, my dearest Lena, you must hold on. What would I ever do without you?"

The sound of footsteps hurrying down the hallway gave her momentary hope. *Oh, please let it be Nicolas!* Julienne prayed silently, wiping the tears from her eyes as the first orange rays of daylight began to creep across the floor of the room toward the bed. The baron crossed the threshold first, moving swiftly aside as the Chevalier d'Argentolle strode in behind him, the room brightening with light as he entered, as if God gave particular sanction to the chevalier's arrival.

Julienne said a silent prayer of thanks, and then willingly relinquished her place. "Dear Lena, it's not the doctor who has come. There's someone special here to see you, someone who I know will bring joy to your heart."

Nicolas rushed to the side of his beloved. He knelt and took her hand in his, despite the presence of Julienne and the baron. Propriety had its proper place, but not now; not when his beloved lay stricken before him. He pressed his lips with aching tenderness against the backside of Sérolène's palm before lifting it to his cheek. Her skin ran hot with fever.

"Séro…my darling Séro…"

Sérolène stared in feverish disbelief, her mouth upturned in a ghostly smile. "How sweet a dream death's approach now brings me."

Her voice sounded so weak, so faint. Tears streamed down Nicolas' cheeks at the almost ghostly sound. He reached out to caress Sérolène's face. "It is no dream, my love. I am here at your side. Where I belong. Where I shall always be."

"You're no phantom of my mind? But how is it possible?"

Nicolas stroked Sérolène's hair, his eyes shining with the fierce light of love. "Your uncle summoned me here. Everyone is much concerned for you, my darling."

"My uncle? Then he knows?"

"How much I love and adore you? Yes, my love. He escorted me to your side. He knows. Everyone knows. How could anyone not see how deeply I love thee?"

Nicolas leaned over Sérolène, anointing her pale feverish visage with his benediction of kisses. "With this kiss I fill you with life and all my love."

Sérolène closed her eyes as his lips pressed against hers, the spark of his ardor reigniting the fading cinder of her life force. Her eyes came open slowly to the sight of a new and unfamiliar world. The dull grey mist, which had seemed to settle over everything, began to clear. The fog of melancholy burned away by the heat of Nicolas' love.

"Oh, my dearest Nico, I've missed you so much. How my heart warms to be with you again."

"As does mine, my angel, but now you must rest. I promise I shall remain at your side as you remained at mine. Sleep now, my dearest, and I shall stay to watch over you."

Nicolas turned toward the baron to ensure his consent, ignoring the pain in his chest and side from the long hard ride and the sleep he had forgone and would continue this day, to eschew.

The baron nodded his acceptance of Nicolas' pledge, putting aside the indiscretion of the chevalier's previous endearments and caresses, and allowing Nicolas the continued indulgence of holding Sérolène's hand as he sat by her side. "We shall arrange things suitably to allow you to remain near her, Monsieur, and in light of the delicacy of the existing situation, we shall elect to overlook certain actions and to treat others with much leniency."

The oath had been spoken. By their own words and their own will, Nicolas and Sérolène bound themselves, one to the other. The baron let out a deep sigh of relief. *No matter what my wife thinks, in light of my niece's importance to all our interests, their betrothal is the best course of action. We now have two fortunes, which depend on the Montferrauds. I must ensure the successful preservation of both, and close the open breach dividing our families.*

"I shall send for Madame Tarnaut and one of the maids to join you, Monsieur, as my dear Julienne is as much in need of rest as my niece. I take my leave for now, fully entrusting in the certitude of your honor. If there is anything you should require to aid your efforts, Monsieur le Chevalier, you have but to ask and we shall do our utmost to comply."

*

Sérolène awoke late in the afternoon, her head no longer pulsing with pain. For the first time in days, she actually felt hungry. She felt the gentle sensation of a hand entwined with her own, and remembering her surprise visitor at dawn, to whom of course it must belong, she turned her gaze toward the side of the bed in expectant delight. A very particular pair of green eyes, tired but cheerful, beamed back at her.

"Welcome back, my darling," Nicolas said.

"Nico? Then it wasn't a dream. You *are* here."

Sérolène's face seemed to glow in the light. Nicolas pressed his lips to her hand in reply. Her skin felt cool to the touch and her eyes no longer appeared sunken and hollow. A new vibrancy suffused her body and spirit. For the first time since Nicolas had begun his bedside vigil, he allowed himself a guarded smile, convinced the crisis had passed.

40

"You've slept through most of the day my love. It is almost evening now. Perhaps you needed the long rest most of all."

Sérolène brought Nicolas' hand to her cheek, pressing it against her lips and anointing it with an endless stream of kisses. "No. What I needed most was you, my dear, sweet, Nico. Your kiss restored my appetite for life."

Nicolas reached over to feel Sérolène's forehead. It too felt cool to the touch. "What about your appetite for food? It has been some time since you took nourishment. Shall I send the maid to bring you something?"

"Now that you mention it, I am rather hungry," Sérolène admitted.

Nicolas turned to address the girl, who sat dozing in the far corner of the room. "Little one, the vicomtesse is hungry. Please go and have something prepared for her, and then inform the rest of the household that she is awake and her fever appears to have broken."

The jet-black young girl, who looked to be no older than eight or nine, awoke with a start at the sound of Nicolas' deep rich voice. "Yes, Monsieur. At once, Monsieur."

She ran off to do as she had been told, leaving Nicolas alone with Sérolène. He wasted no time in finding her lips with his own, then drew back briefly to admire his beloved, awash with relief at the light dancing in her blue-grey eyes.

"I believe your fever is entirely gone, Mademoiselle."

Sérolène reached up to caress his face. "If you kiss me again like that, you'll begin another but much more pleasant one."

The sound of approaching footsteps forced Nicolas to reclaim a more distant and companionable position, though he steadfastly refused to relinquish hold of Sérolène's hand. He had expected just the return of the girl he had sent on an errand, but the room soon filled with visitors as Julienne and Madame Tarnaut entered, followed by the baron himself in the company of Sérolène's physician. Nicolas reluctantly surrendered his physical contact with the vicomtesse, yielding at last to the dictates of propriety as he stood to greet the arriving company. Sérolène sat up in bed under her own power, prompting several excited cries from her new visitors.

Julienne rushed forward first to embrace her *cousine*. "How well you look, dear Lena!"

"Not nearly as well as I feel...now," Sérolène replied, her eyes embracing Nicolas as the baron made the necessary introductions between the chevalier, Madame Tarnaut, and Doctor Saint-Juste, the physician.

The baron approached the bedside with noticeable relief. "I hear your appetite has recovered in league with your spirits, my dear."

Sérolène nodded in reply as the baron put his hand on Nicolas's shoulder with gratitude. "Doctor Saint-Juste has returned as promised to examine the vicomtesse. Monsieur le Chevalier, your escort also arrived some time ago and awaits your instructions. Perhaps you might wish to avail yourself of the opportunity to take some refreshment and to recuperate somewhat after your journey."

A shadow of distress fell across the brow of the vicomtesse at the prospect of being separated from her beloved, no matter how brief, or necessary.

"Must he be gone long, Uncle?"

The baron smiled with indulgence at Sérolène. "I promise you he shall return as soon as possible, my dear."

Nicolas bent to kiss Sérolène's hand. "My men have ridden through the night, Mademoiselle, and I must see to their care. Do not worry, I leave you in much more capable hands than mine, and shall of course return to you with promptness when summoned. Till then I shall remain, as always, steadfast in my devotion to your person and entirely at your command."

The doctor looked on as Nicolas prepared to take his temporary leave. He had the look of one who suspected all along that love had been both the cause and the cure of his patient's ailment.

Only when Nicolas had left the room did he begin to feel the heaviness of his own exhaustion bearing down upon him. He had not slept at all during his long bedside vigil, but while being escorted to the dining room by the baron's servant, François, he began at last to succumb to the effects of his long ride and constant state of anxious wakefulness. Julius stood ready to attend him in the dining room. Nicolas explained the general situation and gave his valet an outline of his plans.

"Tell the Comte de Marbéville I beg the indulgence of our father to allow me to remain here until such time as the vicomtesse should be fully recovered. She saw me through my period of need, now I beg leave to do the same for her. When you return, bring me some suitable changes of clothes for a stay of perhaps one to two weeks."

Julius nodded his understanding.

"How fares my mare?" Nicolas asked with apprehension, knowing how hard he had ridden Gigiana and fearing the worst.

"She gave her all for you, Monseigneur. We could not save her."

Nicolas sighed with regret. "She was a splendid horse, and I very much regret her loss. You may take the rest of the escort home with you. Return when you can, but do not tax yourselves overmuch."

Julius bowed and departed. Exhausted, Nicolas sat alone at the sumptuously laid out table, unable to find the strength or even the desire to partake of the food set out especially for him. He heard the approach of footsteps, but remained as he was, too tired to turn and greet the new arrival.

Julienne entered the dining room behind him. "Please, you must eat something, dear brother."

Nicolas stood at once to render proper courtesies, but instead of offering him her hand, Julienne embraced him with warmth. "Francis told me you were the most noble and honorable of men, dear Nicolas. How right he was. I shall never forget what you have done today, for my dear Lena and for all of us. You have restored the health of my *cousine,* and all our hopes. I only pray it is not too late for my own fortunes to be retrieved," she confessed, sitting to join him at table.

Nicolas regarded Julienne with sympathy, certain she referred to the stalemate which now existed between the families with regard to the completion of her proposed marriage to his brother. "If I may suggest an approach, Mademoiselle?"

"Both my ears and my heart are fully open to you, brother."

"We are fond of the grand *beau geste* in my family. If sincere, it can erase almost all transgressions. If you were able to convince Monsieur and Madame de Salvagnac to pay a visit unannounced to our estate, and if the baronne should then find it convenient to make suitable apology for the treatment meted out to my mother, I am convinced the whole of the situation could still be retrieved to everyone's satisfaction."

Julienne could not conceal how hopeful she felt at Nicolas' suggestion, or what it meant to her. "Does the Comte de Marbéville still reserve a small place for me in his heart, Monsieur?"

Nicolas took a sip of water before answering, his throat dry from his exertions and his long bedside vigil. "Francis is entirely devoted to you, Mademoiselle. I know him better than any, and each day he is separated from you is one in which he perceives the sun to shine with less brightness and warmth. You have made many allies within our household, my mother amongst them. If you can find a means to take the field in defense of your empire, I assure you your friends will rally to your standard. But take the field you must."

Julienne seemed not at all distressed by Nicolas' advice. In fact, she appeared more determined than ever not to give up her own chance for happiness. "I shall do what I can to bring things to bear, Nicolas. I have grown very fond of Francis too. Thank you for restoring my hopes, if nothing else. Now please eat something. While you replenish your strength, I shall see about your accommodations with us, for I do mean to keep you here as long as I can. I warn you, though; you will need all your fortitude to put up with Maman. I beg your forbearance in advance while we accustom her to the necessity and the benefits of your continued presence."

Nicolas bowed with grace, accepting both Julienne's warning and her support. "I shall put myself in your hands, and I shall not deem my mission complete until the vicomtesse is restored to full health and you have reclaimed your former place."

"It pleases me so well, that we are now allies *and* friends. I shall be very glad indeed, when we are at last brother and sister. Eat now while you can, dear brother, and I shall return for you in a short while. For already your Lena craves your presence more than the air she breathes."

Beaux Gestes

The driver slowed his mounts as the heavy carriage approached the elegant row of white marble steps that admitted all guests to the Montferraud château. Before the red and black vehicle had even come to a complete halt, the large double doors of the main entranceway opened inward to disgorge a superb retinue of lackeys and footmen, who fanned out to welcome the visitors as if the sudden arrival of early morning guests had been long anticipated. The attendants wore the signature Montferraud house livery—black shoes, yellow stockings, red breeches, pale blue waistcoats and dark *chasseur* green jackets with yellow facings—brass buttons and linen ruffles at the sleeves and collar. The steward wore breeches of *chasseur* green with a jacket of crimson, the colors reversed to distinguish him from the regular staff. A gauntlet formed to welcome the arrivals, the faces lining each side of the approach, a mix of pigmentation, from almond to midnight black.

The men were handpicked by the marquis himself, selected for the upright quality of their bearing, their experience, and length of service. Al of the men were free, and each earned a daily wage, it being the custom of the marquis to eschew slavery on his plantation, in singular exception to the practices found everywhere else in the colony. Many considered him foolish to pay blacks a wage, others deemed it criminal, but the production of sugar required back breaking and labor-intensive work. Loss of workers through cruelty, neglect, and overwork comprised a large expense for most planters. Why did this wastage persist? Because working enslaved Africans to death and replacing the losses with new arrivals proved simpler than providing proper care and feeding, and also cheaper, provided a ready and plentiful new supply of human chattel could be procured to replace the losses. None of the slave trading powers sought to put an end to such evil profits by outlawing the procurement of African slaves at the source, so cruelty and neglect by plantation owners only fostered more demand for the traffic in human souls.

The marquis had developed a different approach. He treated his workers as important skilled labor. He fed them well, looked after the sick and weak, provided good housing, gave them one day out of seven to rest, and provided clean water to drink. He also allowed them to select their own overseers to administer justice and discipline. As a result, his losses in people and in crops were less than a tenth of what an average plantation suffered, and his profit five to six times the standard yield per acre. No one however, sought to emulate his model of success, built upon greater equity between owner and worker—especially when the workers were black. Instead, the other planters lobbied for stricter edicts to curtail what few rights free blacks still possessed. Some went further and attempted to intimidate the marquis' workers, especially if they left the sanctuary of his estate. The marquis responded by organizing armed patrols, both mounted and on foot, to ensure the safety of his laborers. The borders of his estate were well marked and regularly patrolled. As soon as the red and black carriage crossed the boundary onto his lands, it had been spotted by one of these patrols, and a signal had been sent by torch to the main house, which is why the Baron de Salvagnac's attempt at arriving in complete surprise had been met by such a well-prepared welcoming party.

The Marquis de Blaise sat at table in his green banyan dressing gown and cap. Solomon the house steward brought him the message that the Salvagnac's had been escorted into the *salon de compagnie*. Madame de Blaise sat to the marquis' left, dressed in a red russet silk petticoat and loose fitting house jacket. Francis sat across from his father, attired in a similar manner to the marquis, but wearing a mauve gown and no cap. Only Nicolas, who sat next to Francis, was fully dressed in a dark blue suit, as he often strolled in the gardens directly after breakfast and so always came to morning table fully attired.

"It seems we have unexpected company this morning. Monsieur de Salvagnac and his household have arrived to pay us a visit," the marquis announced to the table in general.

Francis and Nicolas both glanced at Madame de Blaise to gauge her reaction, but she seemed wholly unperturbed by the news. Everyone waited for the marquis to decide what to do. The marquis continued to sit and sip his morning cup of tea, apparently prepared to let the Salvagnacs wait, just as he had been content to let the long-finished marriage contract languish for so many weeks without his signature. "Nicolas, as you are the only one dressed, you shall be our ambassador. Go and welcome our guests and inform them we will all be along in due time."

"Yes, Papa."

The marquis turned his gaze toward Madame de Blaise. "You shall also join us as well, my dear. It's time you were properly introduced to the Salvagnacs and that certain members of that house come to understand who and what you are."

The marquise cast a questioning gaze at her husband, but nodded her acceptance of his orders. "Of course, my dear. If that is your wish."

Francis excused himself to go and dress. He seemed relieved as he rose from the table to go and make ready. After weeks of no visible sign of improvement in the deadlock between the two families, it seemed the baron had finally gathered up enough resolve to act.

While the rest of his family headed toward the private wing of the house to make themselves ready to receive the visitors, Nicolas made his way alone down the long corridor from the dining room to the main salon. Two weeks had passed since he had ridden in haste to attend the sickbed of his beloved, and just several days since he had returned home at the request of the marquis, who had ordered him back to the estate once it became clear the vicomtesse had fully recovered. His stomach churned with nervous anticipation to see Sérolène again. This meeting would be vital for the baron to set matters right, lest the widening breach become irreparable. *Now my fate rests on the outcome as much as my brother's does. Perhaps even more.*

As he passed the vestibule on the west side, Nicolas peered ahead into the room where the guests waited. The *salon de compagnie* extended sixty yards across and forty deep, partitioned into three distinct sections by the artful placement of furniture and decorations, each end of the room bookmarked by a large hearth. The main foyer of the house opened into the central section, which encompassed half the length of the entire space of the room. On the far right near the hearth, a large sectioned off portion, had been purposed for reading and idyll pleasure, with a series of small bookshelves containing several hundred volumes of various Latin, Greek and French works. On the far left of the great room, near the opposite hearth, stood tables and chairs for games and cards. The central section of the salon remained an open rectangle of sofas and couches, with smaller squares of settees love seats and chairs inside the larger enclosure. The whole room could accommodate more than a hundred guests in comfort, with French statuary and busts in the center, Italian marbles on the right, and Greek bronzes and urns on the left. The walls hung with large landscape paintings along the inside length, and portraits of various Montferraud ancestors on the end walls. The back wall held two very large windows which looked out onto the marquis' immaculately manicured and planted gardens. The maroon velvet curtains hanging from the ceiling, which presently hung open to admit the morning light, could be drawn across the room to close off each section. Both right and left sections of the room each had their own hundred-candle chandelier, while the central portion had two chandeliers holding of nearly two hundred candles each.

The ladies were all seated in the central section of the room, facing the pendulum clock to the left of the entranceway. Éléonore and Julienne sat next to their mother on a long sofa. Both wore pale yellow polonaises that looked almost identical. Sérolène sat at right angles to them near her uncle, wearing a bright apple green dress. The baron remained standing beside his wife. She wore a dress of deep blue satin, which complemented the baron's slate grey suit.

Nicolas gathered up his resolve and strode forward, determined not to dwell on everything at stake. The baron turned toward him as soon as he entered the room. Nicolas bowed in greeting and offered the baron his hand.

"Monsieur de Salvagnac, we are honored to receive this unexpected visit."

The baron returned the bow and shook Nicolas' hand with real warmth. "Monsieur d'Argentolle, I'm delighted to see you again."

After Nicolas and the baron exchanged pleasantries, the chevalier moved across the room to greet each of the ladies in turn. Nicolas made a bow of perfect correctness toward the baronne though he could generate little real enthusiasm for his habitual antagonist. "Madame de Salvagnac."

The baronne rose and curtsied in response, extending her hand toward Nicolas. Surprised at this conciliatory gesture, Nicolas was slow to reach out and perform the ritual pressing of lips to flesh, but made up for this momentary lapse by the elegance and charm of his greeting.

The baronne followed up with a guarded but polite smile. "Monsieur le Chevalier, it seems you maintain your habit of rising early, even when at home; a commendable routine."

"I do indeed, Madame. How very kind of you to notice," Nicolas replied.

The baronne's comment seemed almost as many words as she had spoken to Nicolas during the entire length of his stay *chez* Salvagnac, when they had mostly tried to avoid each other; a strategy which had been largely successful for them both, thanks to the help of his future sister in-law, whom Nicolas turned to greet next, with an earnest and welcoming smile. "Mademoiselle de Salvagnac, what a pleasure it is to see you again. Much have I missed your delightful countenance since I returned from your estate."

Julienne beamed back at Nicolas. They had developed a genuine bond of friendship in the wake of Nicolas' second rescue of Sérolène. "I have also regretted your parting as well, Monsieur. Our household hasn't been quite the same, and I've had a more difficult time winning at cards, but I am very pleased to find you so well mended since last I visited with you."

Nicolas bowed again, and then turned to face Éléonore, who giggled with childish delight as his lips touched the back of her hand. Nicolas flashed both dimples at his young favorite. "Mademoiselle Éléonore, how radiant you look today. You are charming beyond measure."

Among the ladies of the Salvagnac household, only Sérolène adored Nicolas more than Éléonore, who seemed still unable to prevent herself from staring fixedly at Nicolas whenever he stood close. "That is very kind of you to say, Monsieur."

The vicomtesse received the last greeting from the chevalier, Nicolas pressing Sérolène's hand to his lips with reverence. "Mademoiselle de La Bouhaire."

Sérolène allowed her gaze to caress Nicolas with affection. "Monsieur d'Argentolle."

What more need he say? No need for long speeches. Their eyes spoke volumes, but only to each other. A simple glance said more than enough.

Nicolas turned to address the general company. He wished to hold onto Sérolène's hand as he spoke. However, the rules of propriety would not allow it. Nevertheless, he could still caress her with his gaze, and he indulged himself most willfully in that pleasure. "Monsieur de Blaise wishes to convey his apologies at not being present to greet you himself. Both he and Monsieur de Marbéville will be along soon to welcome you."

"Will Madame de Blaise not be joining us as well? We had come with the particular hope of paying our respects to the marquise," the baron said.

Nicolas glanced toward Sérolène and Julienne. "Madame de Blaise is of course looking forward to renewing particular acquaintances, and perhaps making new ones."

The baron pressed Nicolas no further, seemingly satisfied with the diplomacy of the chevalier's response. The guests settled in to wait. The baron drew close to a large painting of the Battle of Fontenoy, which dominated the far left wall of the salon, near the Greek section.

The baron stepped close to admire the painting's finer details. "What an extraordinary work. That is your *grand-père,* the elder Marquis de Blaise there, I presume?"

"Yes, Monsieur, at the Battle of Fontenoy, where he died leading the charge that won the day. Though he lies unhorsed and mortally wounded, he still points the way for his regiment to charge."

The painting stood nearly six feet in height and almost double that in length. The baron examined the canvas with interest, examining the direction of the artist's brushstrokes. "I understand you to be particularly fond of horses, Monsieur le Chevalier. So fond, you even enjoy talking to them. Is this true?"

"Yes, on both counts," Nicolas admitted.

"And do they talk back to you?" Madame de Salvagnac teased from her place near the center of the room.

Nicolas turned toward the baronne to reply. "Indeed they do, Madame, but with their actions, which makes them more reliable than most people and easier to comprehend as well."

It wasn't the most generous of responses, but Nicolas did not feel inclined to overlook the baronne's flippancy, given her previous behavior, which had led to the current impasse between both families and the recent collapse of the vicomtesse as well. He wondered how much longer he might have to bear the burden of entertaining everyone all on his own, when he heard the welcome sound of approaching footsteps.

The Montferraud reserves had arrived, the marquis at their head in a bright yellow court suit with amber embroidery. The ladies rose as the marquis walked into the center of the salon. The marquis ignored Madame de Salvagnac and went straight to greet the ladies of his preference. "What an agreeable surprise. How very delighted I am to see you again, Mademoiselle de Salvagnac, Mademoiselle de La Bouhaire."

Madame de Blaise trailed her husband, looking resplendent in a lavender satin gown. She subjected the baronne to the same treatment. The marquise embraced Sérolène, leaning close to whisper in her ear. "Remember this dress, my darling girl? I wore it just for you."

Sérolène beamed at the marquise, exchanging kisses to each cheek. "Of course, Madame. But you wear it better than I could ever hope to."

The marquise's arms found Julienne next. "My dear, dear, girl. We have missed you greatly these many weeks."

She entwined her fingers with Julienne's, and then turned to address the youngest of the visitors. "And how do you do as well, Mademoiselle Éléonore? I'm afraid the last time we met the circumstances were rather less pleasant. Do you remember me at all?"

Éléonore performed her best curtsey and nodded with vigor. "Yes, Madame. I could never forget someone as beautiful as you are. Thank you for looking after me so well when I last visited here."

Madame de Blaise stroked Éléonore's cheek with fondness. "What a delightful child."

"Monsieur and Madame de Salvagnac, may I present to you Madame de Blaise," the marquis said, introducing the marquise.

The baron bowed and kissed the marquise's hand with reverence. Madame de Salvagnac's curtsey however, was ignored, as Francis entered in an orange-brown suit and went straight to greet Julienne and then Sérolène.

"Madame, it is indeed a great honor to make your acquaintance at last. I'm sorry to have missed you when I came to visit the chevalier after the affair in the Cap," the baron said.

"You are too kind, Monsieur de Salvagnac, and you have brought joy to all of us by reuniting us with all of our dear girls."

The baron turned on the charm. "Your kindness in caring for my niece and daughter was beyond measure. You have been an angel of mercy, Madame la Marquise, and I wish to express on behalf of all of us, the very deep extent of our gratitude."

Madame de Blaise inclined her head in acknowledgement of the baron's generous but rather tardy sentiments of appreciation. "We have done what family is compelled by care and affection to do for each other, Monsieur de Salvagnac, nothing more."

"Nevertheless, Madame, we remain indebted to you and wish with all sincerity to acknowledge it," Madame de Salvagnac interjected, determined not to be overlooked any longer.

Silence settled over the room as everyone waited to see how Madame de Blaise would react to this tentative peace offering. The marquise exhaled slowly, the outpouring of her breath audible in the tense stillness, which followed the baronne's words. "I thank you for your considerate...and unexpected words, Madame."

The marquise's even-tempered reply allowed some of the pent-up tension to bleed out of the room. The marquis directed everyone to sit. As hosts and guests took their seats, Monsieur de Salvagnac signaled to two of his lackeys, who stood by the entrance to the vestibule. The lackeys entered, bearing several gifts upon two silver trays.

The baron stood in the center of the salon so he might better direct the presentation of the gifts. "Forgive us for inconveniencing you so early in the day, and on the day after Christmas as well, but I wished to ensure I might find you all at home, so we could present you with these tokens of our esteem."

The marquis tried to protest the baron's generosity as unnecessary, but the baron insisted and at last prevailed upon the marquis to relent. "Julienne, come and give Monsieur de Marbéville his gift."

Julienne rose to present Francis with a handsome bejeweled dress sword, receiving a kiss as reward, to the delighted applause of everyone.

"Come, Éléonore, you're next."

The baron coaxed Éléonore forward, handing her a gift, which she presented to the Marquis de Blaise, an exquisite silver snuffbox carved with hummingbirds and flowers. Éléonore received an embrace and a delicate kiss on the cheek from the marquis in appreciation, which she promptly wiped off, to everyone's laughter.

Madame de Salvagnac rose last. After claiming the last gift on the tray, she turned and advanced with hesitation toward Madame de Blaise. "Madame de Blaise, I should like to beg the favor of presenting you with a small gift I have chosen," the baronne began haltingly, her former air of haughty pride stripped from her speech and her manner.

Despite the humility of her approach, the marquise seemed reluctant to accept any gift from the baronne, given the hotness of their last encounter and the fault the baronne bore for engendering it. The baronne sensed this, and performed a deep curtsey before the marquise, inclining her head with a humble and penitent air. "I know I have no right to expect your indulgence, Madame. I should expect rather your censure in light of how dreadfully I behaved toward you. Nevertheless, I do beseech thee most humbly to grant me this undeserved favor."

Nicolas watched in awestruck silence. Francis stood behind Julienne. He looked at Nicolas and gave an approving nod of the head.

The baronne cast a gentle look toward her husband. "I have lived much of my life in small circles of acquaintance, from which I acquired many habits and opinions. Some good, and some, I confess, quite mistaken. I have in the past few weeks taken much time to reflect upon my conduct the last time I had the honor to visit this house, Madame. After all the courtesies you have shown, and after all the chevalier risked for us, I cannot look back upon my actions without feeling a profound sense of shame and remorse."

A collective state of shock descended upon the room as the baronne paused to gather her composure. None seemed more surprised than Julienne and Sérolène, to see the baronne in so contrite and penitent a state of self-reflection.

The baronne set her gift down upon a small end table. Her hands visibly trembled as she reached out to take Madame de Blaise's hands in her own. "Shame, that I had not the wisdom to look beyond my mistaken point of view to see you for the extraordinary woman you are. Remorse, Madame, because I had not the strength of character to write to you and beg your forgiveness for the wrongs I have done you, as I do now with complete contrition, in front of all those dearest to me."

A solitary tear fell from the baronne's cheek to stain the blue satin fabric of her gown. No scene could have been better conceived or acted out; no better effect wrought upon the entire assembled party.

Quel beau geste! Nicolas observed, admiring the splendid performance of the baronne. The marquis nodded his head slightly in the direction of the marquise.

Madame de Blaise rose from her seat and embraced Madame de Salvagnac with tenderness. "How generous your words, and how warm your heart. I assure you I have wished for nothing more than the happiness of all."

The baronne retrieved her gift and presented it to the marquise. "This small gift expresses the heartfelt esteem and affection we all have come to have for you and your family. It is a mere trifle in comparison to the true depth of our gratitude. I have made a most grievous mistake in neglecting your friendship. I hope you find it in your heart to forgive me, and I assure you from this day forward, I wish only for us to become the best of friends."

Madame de Blaise embraced the baronne again. "You and your family have ever been dear to my heart. Be assured, Madame, you may always count upon me as your friend."

At the prompting of the baronne, the marquise began unwrapping the gift's silk outer covering to reveal a velvet jewelry case, which held a stunning emerald necklace interlaced with diamonds, the piece carefully chosen to match the color of Madame de Blaise's eyes. It looked to be worth a small fortune, and the marquise seemed visibly affected, though more by the sentiment than the value of the gift. She embraced the baronne a third time in thanks, and performed an elegant curtsey toward Baron Salvagnac, which he returned with a low bow of his own. The baron beamed at his wife from across the room, as the marquise and the baronne walked arm and arm to sit together.

The marquis then came forward to shake hands with the baron. The breach between the two families had been closed. "I shall complete the remaining details in the agreement and affix my signature to the contract of marriage today, Monsieur. If it is not too inconvenient, perhaps we might conduct the ceremony in the next few days. I should not like to enter the New Year without assuring our children of the happiness we have promised them."

The marquis looked across the room at Julienne, who glowed with happiness as she stood next to Francis. The baron's face reflected his delight that the most pressing of his affairs had met with a satisfactory conclusion. "Of course, Monsieur le Marquis. Whatever you find most convenient shall be done."

The general mood turned gay and carefree, spurred on by the evident affection on display between the soon-to-be newlyweds and the state of open cordiality prevailing between the marquise and the baronne. An hour passed pleasantly by, and then another. Perhaps feeling that enough had been done, the baron stood to depart.

"My dear family, though we have much enjoyed being in your company, I regret that my wife and I have pressing matters elsewhere which require our presence."

Everyone stood to see the Salvagnacs off. Madame de Blaise seemed the most affected by the baron's plans to depart so early. "Must you take everyone with you? Perhaps you could leave the children with us for some time—we promise to have them home by nightfall."

"Oh, please, Papa, can we?" Éléonore pleaded.

The baron smiled down at Éléonore. "I shall leave the decision up to Madame de Salvagnac. For it is well known, my dear little one, that I am entirely unable to refuse you anything."

All heads turned toward the baronne for her decision.

"If my husband is unable to refuse, how can my softer heart possibly do so?" the baronne said.

Éléonore laughed with delight, tugging on Nicolas' hand with glee.

The baron turned to beckon Nicolas to his side. "Nicolas, my boy! Would you do me the honor of accompanying me as we walk to the carriage?"

Nicolas gently released himself from Éléonore's grasp to accompany the baron, the rest of the party following them out. Nicolas and the baron walked side by side, preceded by a footman. The baron halted as they reached the main entrance and turned to speak to Nicolas and the rest of the party. "You will pardon me for waiting so late, Monsieur le Chevalier, to present you with your gift. I can assure you,

you were not forgotten in our thoughts. Indeed, how could we forget someone to whom we owe so much?"

Nicolas glanced toward Sérolène. "You have done more than enough for me as it is, Monsieur. Your consideration already outstrips my ability to repay you."

The baron patted Nicolas on the shoulder. "Forgive me, but I must be allowed to disagree. Monsieur de Blaise, I beg you to permit me your indulgence in this last gift. As you will see, I had some trouble in procuring exactly what I desired. It has been my little secret. Not even Madame de Salvagnac knew of it, though the observations of my niece and others who know the chevalier well have influenced me greatly in my choice."

"You have me at a disadvantage, Monsieur, but I am happy to yield, nevertheless," the marquis said.

The baron smiled and bowed his head to acknowledge the marquis' acceptance. He turned to address Nicolas again directly. "What can one give in recompense to someone who has sacrificed so much, risking his life unselfishly to save the lives of others? What can one do to reward the suffering such a young man went through, not only in the Cap, but also in the weeks afterward in recovery? I asked many questions about you during this time, Monsieur, with the purpose of better understanding the type of man you are. The answers I received had all but convinced me of the substance of your character. The swiftness with which you answered our plea when my niece faced danger only convinced me of the correctness of my opinions. I know how dearly you care for your horses and that the grey mare rated as your favorite. To have ridden such a splendid animal to death in order to come to our aid was selfless and noble, I tell you. How you must have regretted her loss. Here is my attempt to make it up to you."

The baron bid the footman open the door, and as the light streamed in, he led the party into the courtyard. Tethered next to the baron's carriage stood the two most beautiful horses Nicolas had ever seen.

"Voilà! Here is my gift to you. These are the best horses Alsace has to offer. The black stallion, I'm told, is matchless but temperamental. He's thrown three riders already who tried to break him, but he is afraid of nothing and will run and jump to exhaustion for anyone who can master him. He is a token of our thanks for your heroism in the Cap. The grey mare is docile and friendly and can fly like the wind. She is a measure of our gratitude for the sacrifice of your own mare. They are both for you, my boy, with my heartfelt thanks."

Nicolas stood speechless, glancing toward his father for approval that he could actually accept the splendid pair of horses. The marquis nodded and Nicolas cried out with joy, propriety thrown to the winds as he turned and hugged the baron in gratitude.

The baron laughed happily. It seemed plain from the looks of all those gathered, that he had quite outdone himself. Everyone stared in admiration at the magnificent mounts, which must have cost a small fortune to find and procure. The horses were untethered by the grooms and paraded before the gathering so they could be admired. The black stallion required three handlers as he reared and stomped in annoyance.

"Saddle them both at once," Nicolas instructed the equerries.

Madame de Blaise turned toward the marquis, her eyebrows raised in doubt. "Do you think that wise, my dear?"

"No. But it is audacious and in keeping with his nature, and so we shall leave him to his task," the marquis declared.

The equerries saddled both mounts. Nicolas boldly approached the snorting stallion, the great black head looming high above him as the horse reared up on its hindquarters. "Release him."

The equerries looked toward the marquis, who nodded his assent. Nicolas took the bridle in hand as the handlers stepped back. He moved in close to stroke the jet-black horse on the head, until it lowered its nose enough for him to whisper into its ear. Whatever words he spoke appeared to calm the great beast. Satisfied he and the horse now understood each other; Nicolas mounted up with the aid of one of the grooms. As soon as he sat on the stallion's back, it reared as if to throw him, but Nicolas leaned into the stallion's neck and laughed in unfettered glee. Urging the horse on with his riding crop, he then shot off like a thunderbolt, quickly disappearing from sight as he rode off at the gallop.

After several minutes and no sign of either horse or rider, there followed some discussion as to what to do, led by the worried looking mother of the bold young rider. "Perhaps we should send the men after him? Was he really riding that fearsome stallion or has it simply run off with him?"

Francis pointed in the distance. "Look there, Madame. I believe you have your answer."

Nicolas came up the road at a trot, guiding the horse from side to side on precise diagonals as though on parade. It seemed clear that the great beast had accepted him willingly as master.

As Nicolas rode up to the assembled company, he performed a neat pirouette in the courtyard before dismounting, a wide grin of satisfaction brightening his face. Nicolas slapped his thigh with his riding crop. "Extraordinary! What a magnificent animal! Splendid!"

The baron applauded Nicolas' success. "You've broken the stallion. Well done. Now you must try the mare."

Nicolas complied at once, putting the dappled grey mount through its paces in the courtyard, finding her to be all the baron had promised and a little more. After Nicolas dismounted, the horses were led to the stables. As the Montferrauds and the Salvagnac ladies looked on from the wide marble steps, Monsieur and Madame de Salvagnac said their farewells and mounted the carriage to depart. The baron craned his head out of the carriage window to motion Nicolas forward.

The baron leaned out to speak to Nicolas as he approached the side of the carriage. "Tell me Nicolas, if I may be so familiar as to address you by your given name. What did you say to the stallion to make him obey?"

Nicolas whispered in the baron's ear. The baron laughed, and then waved his goodbyes as the four-horse team started off.

Madame de Salvagnac looked across the coach at her husband. "Well, what did he say that could be so amusing?"

"He said, 'I told him, if he did not embarrass me in front of my lady, I would not embarrass him in front of his.'"

The peals of the baronne's laughter rose above the steady thumping of the horses' hooves, as the coach made its way out of the courtyard and receded into the distance.

Decisions of Import

On New Year's Eve, in front of a small party of family and witnesses, Julienne Rocheforte de Salvagnac took her vows before God and became a Montferraud and Comtesse de Marbéville. The marriage rite took place in the Montferraud's own private chapel, followed by a celebratory meal with family and a select group of important guests. Among those in attendance at the ceremony were the Comtesse de Talonge, the Comte d'Argout, Monsignor Arnaud and the Vicomte de Tollaincourt. A separate and much grander service would take place in late spring or early summer in Paris, where the entire event could be properly stage-managed. Following this second ceremony in France, the Montferrauds and the Salvagnacs would take up permanent residence in the city of light, in order to exploit the fruits of the new alliance.

Paris presented both opportunity and danger. With the Comte de Marbéville's prospects settled, the marquis resolved to decide on Nicolas' future before the family embarked for France. There were several possible choices to consider. For some time, Monsignor Arnaud had tried to convince the marquis to commit Nicolas to a future in the Church. It seemed the logical choice for the boy, given the unusual circumstances of Nicolas' background, but the marquis appeared reticent to force Nicolas to live a life of celibacy and contemplation, given his son's vibrant nature and immense physical gifts.

Nicolas' budding relationship with the Vicomtesse de La Bouhaire, and the avid intervention of the marquise in support of the young lady who had become a special favorite, only reinforced the marquis' belief that paths other than the spiritual path beckoned for Nicolas. But would the baron consent to see his niece promised to Nicolas? And should Blaise himself agree to such an alliance, when there might be more promising candidates from the perspective of the wider family interests? The marquis felt he had delayed long enough. Now he had to decide.

*

The marquis rode side by side with Nicolas, making a rough circle around the five-thousand-hectare estate. To avoid being plagued by swarms of insects, they maintained a quick and steady pace, riding briskly through cane fields and alongside planted orchards. The horses sweated profusely in the heat, and after reaching the half way point of the circuit, both horses and riders needed a brief respite.

The marquis reined in under the shade of a moss-encrusted Jacaranda tree. He removed his hat and fanned himself against the heat, allowing his horse to rest and graze on the thick grass underfoot. "What a pleasant New Year's Day it's turned out to be, though rather warm for my tastes. You have entered the time of your manhood, Nicolas. I sense this year will prove much more eventful than last. I think now is an opportune time to inform you of the decisions I've made with regard to your future."

Nicolas nodded his head in silence, too nervous to do anything but stare down at the highly polished sheen of his father's high brown riding boots. The marquis sat astride a chestnut mare, resplendent in tan leather breeches and a dark green riding coat of light cotton, which made the heat more bearable. Nicolas sat astride the grey mare the baron had gifted him, which he had named Aemilia. His boots were knee-high and black, to match the color of his riding coat. Soft chamois leather breeches, bleached almost white, encased thighs as thick as the trunk of the tree that sheltered them. Nicolas removed his three-cornered hat to swat away a passing wasp attracted to the white feather plume.

"I am dispatching you to Martinique for special training in swordsmanship, arms, and horsemanship. Francis will escort you and see to the particular introductions, as he is a patron of sorts of the place to which you are to be sent. The training will be very arduous. There is much to learn and only a short time to complete your studies. Your preparation will be accelerated to the maximum so you absorb everything needed. You will be taxed to the limits of your capacities. It will be difficult, but it *is* necessary. How will that suit you, Monsieur?"

Nicolas looked up to meet his father's gaze. "It will suit me very well, Papa."

The marquis nodded, pleased that Nicolas accepted the arduous prospect outlined for him. It boded well that he seemed willing to work and to suffer; habits too many young men of rank had long ago abandoned. But their house, long bred to war, understood that suffering could be both rewarding, and useful.

"Will I be gone long, Papa?"

"That depends upon your ability to absorb the instruction you will undertake, and on the availability of the ships we require to take us to France."

"I see. Will I be going with you to France, Papa?"

"You will. I have decided you will attend the École Militaire in Paris."

Nicolas understood at what the decision meant. He would enter the Army after all. The marquis gave Nicolas a wry grin. "It seems you enjoy your intellectual jousts with Monsignor Arnaud, but your mother tells me the prospect of a celibate life inside the cloister holds no appeal. I suppose you'd prefer a life outside the monastery, with a wife and children of your own."

Nicolas nodded. "I would indeed, Papa. When do you think we'll depart? And are the Salvagnacs coming as well?"

"No earlier than March, so you'll have at least three months to complete your new studies, but precisely when is anyone's guess. The fleet is rather busy off the coast of North America now, and so we must wait until fortune should choose to smile upon our efforts in the war and thereby provide us with suitable escort. And yes, the Salvagnacs are coming as well, and your vicomtesse."

Nicolas brightened visibly at this last revelation. The marquis dismounted. Nicolas did the same. They walked their mounts to the top of a small hill, which gave them a pleasing overlook of the entire estate. The château sat long and squat in the distance, the symmetry of its grounds and gardens a splendid view to behold even at the range of several miles. The rest of the vista teemed lush and green, colored by the thousands of acres of sugar cane that made up the majority of the estate's crop. A crop that necessitated a small army of laborers to till it.

Nicolas took a mouthful of water from the pouch attached to his shoulder belt. "It's beautiful, isn't it, Papa?"

The marquis squinted in the direction of the field hands, their figures like dark insects in the distance. *All of this will be lost.* He knew it in the pit of his soul, but his fellow Frenchmen, in their blind pride and obstinacy couldn't see the storm that lay ahead. *No man will live forever in bondage. The enslaved will rise up and take their freedom. As they must. As any man must.* Still, it was indeed a magnificent view and tomorrow's troubles seemed very far away.

"Yes, it is. It could be a paradise on earth, but instead it's become a living hell of corruption and barbarity. That is what slavery makes of things, my boy, and why I have decided to sell all my holdings here when we return to France."

Blaise glanced at Nicolas, whose features clouded with doubt and surprise. Nicolas had never known another home and looked crestfallen to hear that the estate would be sold. "I know you are astonished to hear it, but I must act now to preserve our future fortunes. I don't think this place will last another generation before it begins to collapse from the weight of its accumulated sins. The blacks will rise up as they must to gain their freedom, and those remaining who have enslaved them will then know what it is like to feel the lash...and worse."

Nicolas listened in silence to the bleak prognosis from his father. Then he turned toward the marquis, his eyes cast down in thought. "I suppose I never really considered the plight of the enslaved blacks, nor their future. I pitied them, of course, but can things really be any different?"

"Of course they can, Nicolas. In fact, they must. Slaveholding corrupts not only those held in bondage, but those holding the chains as well. For what man will work when he can force another to do it for him? And without work, we become soft, lazy and degenerate, with nothing to do but seek our own pleasure."

Nicolas nodded in agreement. "You're right, Father. Why shouldn't they fight? I certainly would, were I in their place. But must you also leave this place, even though you own no slaves? Your workers are free men, every one. Surely you'd be safe if you decided to remain here."

The marquis' countenance grew somber as he stared off into the distance. "When the uprising comes, the only thing which will matter will be the color of one's skin. We Frenchmen have butchered black Africans in countless hundreds of thousands, Nicolas. Even if they could forgive us so great a crime, they could never forget it. Perhaps in time it will be possible to live and work together as free men and equals, but I fear the happy prospect of such a day lies in a far distant future—one neither of us will live to see. This island will weep rivers of blood when the reckoning comes, and it will come sooner than many here believe possible. No one will be safe."

"No one? What will become of your workers when we leave, Papa? Will they still have a place, or a future here?"

"I shall offer to pay the passage for those who wish it, to any territory, French, or other, where they can maintain their freedom. It's the least I can do after the hazards they have braved for us."

Nicolas frowned. "I don't understand, Papa. Haven't you also borne your share of risk by freeing them and accepting other free men as workers? In addition to the tax of manumission, you've also paid the *taille* and absorbed an unfair share of the *corvée* for them as well."

The marquis sighed at the bitter necessity of having to explain to his son the realities of how the world truly worked. "Yes, I have paid taxes and upkeep and done what I could to improve their dwellings, but those who work our lands have risked far more than I. They cannot go into town or stray far from my lands for fear of vigilante reprisals against them. Though they are free, they are virtual prisoners here. Shall I relate to you the full horror of two of the families who tried to go to the Cap to sell some of the produce from their small plots? Suffice it to say they never made it there. The men and two young boys were found strung up in trees along the road, tortured before they were hanged, their privates removed and placed in their mouths, their bodies burned. The oldest boy was three years younger than you are now. What they did to the women is unspeakable."

Nicolas' frowned with disgust. "Why were the criminals not found and brought to justice, Father?"

The marquis spat on the ground. "The perpetrators *were* justice, Nicolas. They are all members of the local police and judiciary, acting on behalf of the planters. That is what can be expected of His Majesty's representatives here and why I have my own armed men to patrol our lands. What we have reaped on this island, is the poisonous spawn of centuries of despotism and all it breeds—contempt for humanity, life, the law—the only things which matter are privilege, rank and title. Honor and justice—these are just empty words whose substance has long been forgotten."

The marquis looked hard at his son, the shadow of his own culpability lingering over his furrowed brow. "I've been a part of the problem Nicolas. Now with Francis married and you soon to reach manhood, the future of our line is secured. I've hidden myself away here too long, bound by an old compact of honor. It is time I went back and assumed my rightful place at court, no matter the risks. That is the only way I can help to bring about the changes we need to save France. For more than a thousand years we have fought for France and the ideal she represented, long before the name of Bourbon ever assumed the royal crown. The name Frank means freedom. Since ancient times, the vile practice of slavery has been outlawed in our borders, but now, in these lands we have conquered, we turn a blind eye to the corrupting traffic in flesh, and for nothing more than profit. We have forgotten the meaning of what France really is Nicolas. It is the light that shines in the darkness of Europe—

ever eternal, ever free—beacon to knowledge, the arts and all the best hopes of man. This is the glory, for which we, the ancient chevaliers fight. Never forget that. If this creaking despotism endangers her, it must be swept aside. The entire rotten edifice must be brought down until none of it remains. Always remember, Nicolas, we were knights long before there were kings."

*

The marquis' words shocked Nicolas. He had always considered himself and his family to be loyal subjects of the King, but his father's words hinted at a truer and more ancient alliance. His mind raced with the implications of this new viewpoint. The essence of nobility encompassed more than the sum of hereditary rights and privileges. True nobility ran much deeper than birthright or blood. *France is our glory, and she is freedom!*

"I understand, Papa. I promise whatever you decide, I'll be ready to do as you ask when the time comes."

Nicolas realized something important had occurred—a rite of passage, whether intended or not. He looked outward at the vast lush world laid before him. It seemed different somehow. The prism through which he had envisioned the world and his own circumstances had been irrevocably altered by his father's words. Though he had not moved an inch, the place he had stood upon just moments before had disappeared, along with his youthful illusions, and he could never go back to seeing things in the same way.

Nicolas looked across at his father and saw him anew as well, not as a mythical colossus, but a man just like himself. Older, wiser perhaps, with vastly more experience, but smaller than himself now, the signs of age beginning to appear in his face and body—though his true power remained immense. For the first time they had spoken to each other with real candor on so many substantive affairs. And his father had treated him not as a child to be lectured to, but as a man. The realization prompted Nicolas to act as a man and take the marquis into his most private circle of confidence.

"Papa, I'd like to speak to you about something very important."

The marquis nodded his encouragement. "Go on."

Nicolas clenched the reins in his left hand. Aemilia shifted her feet behind him, sensing his anxiety. "I'm desperately in love with Mademoiselle de La Bouhaire, and I believe her feelings to be equal to my own in every way. I would gladly do anything in my power if you should consent to a match between us. Would you agree to speak to Monsieur de Salvagnac on my behalf?"

The seconds that followed seemed an eternity. Nicolas could barely endure the interval of silence, fearing a negative reaction from his father, which would doom his hopes entirely. Aemilia lowered her head to graze on the nearby flowers and grass, completely indifferent to his plight. Nicolas raised his eyes toward his father, who would now determine the direction of his entire life, for good…or ill.

The corners of the marquis' mouth turned up in a wry grin. "Of course you are. It's quite obvious to anyone who cares to look that providence has intended you two for each other. I've already made up my mind to discuss it with Salvagnac. He's due here in two days to settle some outstanding matters between us. I suppose we shall have to add your futures to our list of things to discuss."

Nicolas could scarcely believe his ears, or his immense good fortune. "Thank you, Papa. But do you think the baron will agree to it?"

"Not without extracting a suitable price. He's a banker, my boy. He'll want to obtain the most value he can get for his niece," Blaise said, with more honesty than perhaps Nicolas might have wished.

The marquis seemed to see the shadow of worry darken Nicolas' face. "Come, come now, no long faces. Have you forgotten who your father is? You need only do as I instruct and you shall obtain the thing you desire. I know what Monsieur de Salvagnac values most, and more importantly, what Madame de Salvagnac cannot resist. They will not refuse me. Upon this you may be sure."

The marquis mounted his horse. Nicolas grinned wide, exposing both sets of dimples and a row of perfect white teeth, and then mounted up as well. The marquis glanced at his son from the saddle, allowing himself a brief expression of indulgent parental pride, perhaps at what a handsome lad he had sired, then sat up straight and tall in the saddle. "Now, Monsieur d'Argentolle, since you wish to pay court like a man, let's see if you can really ride like one!"

*

His challenge issued, the marquis whirled his horse about and galloped back down the trail toward their château. Nicolas laughed, turned his grey mare, and followed in pursuit. They rode hard for several miles, straining themselves and their horses to the limit to see who would be first to reach the gatepost marking the carriage road which led up to the château.

With less than a mile to go, Nicola had a commanding lead. Aemilia proved as swift as the baron had promised, and an even better jumper, which allowed Nicolas to take shortcuts, leaping over hedges and streams the marquis could not negotiate. Galloping close to the edge of the woods which marked the outside boundary of their estate, the young chevalier approached the last stretch of open meadow with the finish line of the gateposts well in sight.

Ahead of Nicolas lay the main road to the château and victory. He had only to ride straight up to take it, but recent rains left the lane well rutted and in questionable condition for the passage of horses and vehicles. Instead, he followed the alternate path of a deep gulley that paralleled the main thoroughfare, intending to come up close to a small ford with more secure footing, and then cross to the other side.

Nicolas breached the crest of the hill at the gallop. Glancing over his shoulder, he grinned with satisfaction. The marquis followed at a considerable distance behind him. He had won. A shadow flashed at the edge of his vision. Nicolas jerked the reins hard to the left.

"Wheel!"

The action came almost too late. Aemilia narrowly avoided a collision with an oncoming rider who came up out of the muddy depression on the reverse crest of the hill. Distracted by ruminations of victory and a successful appeal to the baron, Nicolas had almost run straight into disaster as he crested the incline, but the qualities of his mount and his able horsemanship had spared him a potentially dangerous fall. The other rider, who had also been galloping hard, proved not as skillful. Both the rider and horse took a bad fall into the streambed. The fallen mount regained its footing but the rider remained on the ground. Four other horsemen galloped up over the crest, reining in at the sight of their fallen comrade.

The centermost rider motioned for two of the horsemen to dismount and provide aid to their fallen comrade. "*Foutre,* but you're a clumsy bastard! I'll have the skin flayed from your hide for your careless stupidity!"

The man who spoke wore rough leather breeches, low riding boots, a shirt with no waistcoat or jacket, and a wide brimmed straw hat. A sword hung at the man's left side, which marked him as a gentleman of some sort, despite the poor quality of his dress. The man's rank mattered, as did his lack of manners. He seemed the obvious leader of the posse.

Another of the riders had the look of an Indian, with long straight hair, which ran down past his shoulders. The other two were rough and hard boiled, with an air of experience and trouble about them. They were the type of tough plantation brutes who took pleasure in meting out abuse. Bloodstains dotted the shirts and breeches of all the riders, as if they'd just assisted in butchering an animal. Most would have found them an imposing and fearful sight, and elected to give way, but Nicolas had no part in most. His blood still surged hot from the excitement of the ride and the narrow avoidance of a fall. The insolence of the man's address also stirred his ire.

Rather than yield, Nicolas turned his mount toward the speaker, jerking his head in the direction of the fallen horseman. "It seems the clumsy fellow is over there. And if you do not learn to keep a civil tongue, you will soon join him, minus that stinking pile of shit on your shoulders which I suppose in your case passes for a head."

Nicolas' right hand grasped the hilt of his sword, ready to avenge the previous affront to his honor. The man looked

Nicolas up and down. He seemed astonished to be challenged by such a stripling. "Arrogant whelp. I'll see you lying broken in the mud at my feet. A just vengeance for the injury you've done to my son. I'll take your fine grey horse too as settlement for the trouble you've caused."

The man with the sword pointed his riding crop at Nicolas. "Quinot. You and Mordu, teach this gibbering ape a lesson!"

Had the posse leader possessed even the smallest degree of shrewdness he would have realized that servants on St. Domingue were not allowed to carry swords, nor did they ride mounts worth more than the yearly output from an average plantation. But Gerrard Petitfleur never possessed astuteness in any measurable amount.

The thick-faced Quinot moved toward Nicolas. He grinned wide, showing a mouth full of blackened, rotting teeth, then pulled his pistol from his belt, his thumb already pressing back the cock as he prepared it to fire. Dimwitted as he appeared, he seemed to take his master's orders to mean the lesson must be fatal.

Nicolas saw the mortal danger at once. He pivoted his mare in a tight arc to the right and drew his sword in the same motion. Aemilia felt the bite of spurs in her flanks and shot forward. It took less than two seconds for Quinot to raise his arm. Far too much time. Aemilia swallowed the distance. Nicolas' rapier pierced through the big brute's heart. Quinot's dead hand fired into empty air.

Nicolas remained in motion. He wheeled behind the dead man's horse to extricate his blade, leaning hard left in the saddle. Aemilia turned back toward her starting point and reached it in three long strides. Petitfleur had drawn his sword. A second and last mistake. Nicolas came into contact range, parried the attempted thrust and sliced obliquely upward at the throat. Aemilia's impetus provided all the force he needed. The blade passed clean through the neck, exiting in a graceful arc above Nicolas's shoulder.

For several seconds, Gerrard Petitfleur and his severed head remained upright. Then the movement of his mount caused the head to fall backward to the ground. The mouth hung open, shouting an order no one would ever hear. The eyes stared wide in death. Petitfleur's horse bolted, carrying the headless corpse with it.

Nicolas wheeled again to confront the rider named Mordu, who had unslung his musket from its saddle sling and attempted to prime it to fire. Nicolas charged straight toward him, thrusting across his body and down. The point of his blade pierced Mordu through his left eye and continued onward through the brain. A foot of steel burst through the back of the overseer's head. The lifeless corpse fell backward, musket still in hand, the head impaled to the earth by Nicolas' sword.

Weaponless save for the small dagger he carried in his belt, Nicolas charged down the Indian, the last man standing, who stood halfway between the fallen rider and his own horse. The Indian's long black hair flowed easily in the breeze that came up over the rise of ground. He crouched down for a moment, as if weighing flight or further resistance, but the skirmish was already lost.

The marquis arrived at the gallop and reined in hard, surveying the situation before him. Three of the trespassing riders were dead, a fourth held at bay by the threat of Aemilia's raised hooves. The last rider, who looked little older than Nicolas, lay upon the ground, prostrate and still as death. The marquis snarled in outrage at finding trespassers on his lands. Trespassers who had been armed and from the looks of things, had dared to attack his son.

"What is the meaning of this? How dare you shoot at us, and on my own lands! By God, I shall see you hang for this!" Blaise shouted.

"This surly fellow here is to blame for what happened. Our party rode in hot pursuit of some runaway slaves when that fellow came across our path and caused my master's son to lose control of his horse and fall. When my master admonished him, he insulted us in a manner most vile. Our honor could not allow such an affront to proceed…"

The marquis visibly seethed. "Your honor? Your honor! What honor has a churl like you to speak of? And to whom do you think you are speaking, by God?"

The long-haired rider defiantly stood his ground. "My master Monsieur Petitfleur owns a plantation not far from here at La Porte. He was an important gentleman among the planters. You would do well to cooperate and to mind your tone. I imagine the authorities will take much interest in the circumstances of his death."

The marquis spat his displeasure onto the earth, a sign that he had borne enough insolence for one day. "How dare you presume to threaten me? I am the Marquis de Blaise. All of you are intruders here and subject to my justice. You have trespassed upon my lands, insulted my family, and compounded your crimes with a brazen attack upon my son, who is a nobleman of France. An attack, which I witnessed with my own eyes. If I decide not to hang you today myself, I shall recommend to the governor that all your master's lands and property be forfeited as reparation for the insults you have given, and that you be put in the stocks and publicly flogged as an example!"

Tibohio, the Indian, blanched. He dropped to one knee and lowered his head, aware now of the magnitude of the error his master had committed in seeking to mete out his own summary justice. A few paces away, the disembodied head of Monsieur Petitfleur stared at him accusingly in death, as if protesting his quick surrender.

"Please, Monseigneur! I did not know to whom I spoke and humbly ask for your pardon. It is the shock of seeing my master killed before my very eyes that drove me to speak as I did. I beg you, Monseigneur, to have mercy. Punish me, if you must, but spare my master's family. The young master has a mother and three sisters to look after now. What shall we do if we lose our plantation?"

The marquis considered the plea for clemency as he continued to seethe. Tibohio said a soft prayer of thanks to the nuns at the orphanage who raised him, for insisting he speak untainted French.

The marquis looked toward Nicolas. "As the Chevalier d'Argentolle is the one most aggrieved by your conduct, I shall leave it to him to decide your fate."

Nicolas looked at his father in surprise. The marquis' gaze did not waver. Nicolas had to decide. He turned to regard the bodies of the fallen men, his stomach now turning at the realization that he had actually killed. Yes, he had dueled many times before, but none of those encounters had been fatal. He felt no pleasure in what he had done, even though he had acted to save his own life. His anger still burned at how he had been spoken to, but he considered what his feelings might have been, had his own father been lying in the dirt before him.

What of the boy's family? Must they all now suffer the loss not only of a father, but of their livelihood as well? He couldn't bring himself to order such a thing, even though he knew that any mercy shown might not be appreciated by the young Petitfleur when he regained consciousness. Nicolas suspected rather, that he had gained a lifelong enemy.

Nicolas dismounted to retrieve his sword. Now that the danger had passed, he felt the weight of what he had done in his arms and in the pit of his stomach. "Take your dead and return to your lands. I bear no grudge against anyone."

Nicolas put his foot securely on the chest of the man he had slain. He grasped the hilt and pulled it from the lifeless skull, wiping the bits of brain and flesh that clung to the blade, on the dead man's shirt. "But I warn you, my benevolence comes at a price. Should you or those you serve ever insult me or my family again, my retribution will be swift and merciless. I will not begin a quarrel between us, but if one should arise, for any reason, I promise you, I shall be the one to end it. Make sure your young master well understands this."

The deadly hiss of his sword returning to its scabbard sealed Nicolas' promise. He remounted his horse. The marquis looked at the Indian. "Your sentence has been pronounced. See that you mark it well. I shall send a wagon down to help you carry your dead and wounded, as it appears your new master will be unable to ride. Remember well these woods. They mark the outer boundaries of our lands. See that you respect them the next time you come this way."

The marquis turned his horse and spurred it on in the direction of the road to the château. Nicolas followed behind his father, the race and its challenge wholly forgotten. When they arrived at the estate, the marquis gave instructions to send a wagon down to carry away the dead. He also dispatched a party of armed guards to escort the unwanted visitors off his lands.

*

Once inside the estate, the marquis led Nicolas into the empty *salon de compagnie*. He could see the turmoil on his son's face, it relieved him that his son felt no glory in the taking of human life. Yes, killing was sometimes necessary, but taking another life should never be something one ought to develop a taste for.

"Today you have had three trials, Nicolas, and you have learned the most important responsibilities of a seigneur—to dispense life and death with honor, tempered by justice and mercy."

Nicolas turned toward his father. He looked as if he might be sick on the spot. The marquis knew from his own experiences that the bitter aftertaste of killing could be a hard thing to keep down.

"Do you think this will be the end of it, Papa?"

The marquis shook his head. "The end of it? On the contrary. I've a feeling your story with the Petitfleurs is just beginning. As you have pledged your word not to strike first, you must be well prepared to absorb the first blow. I assure you when it does come, it will be delivered during a moment calculated to do you the greatest harm."

Blaise crossed over to the hearth to regard with pride, the young man who had this day proven that his heart, his arm, and his reason were mature beyond the span of his years. "Do you know what it is that makes us noble, Nicolas? The law and custom say it is our pedigrees, but our blood is the least noble thing we have. What makes us truly noble is how we act. For us, honor must not be just a word. It is how we live. The sword is our scepter of justice, but its use must always be properly tempered. Today you have become a man. You have bested me on horseback, a thing not many can achieve, and you have spoken like a man of your love and your future. You have also taken lives—justly perhaps, but more importantly, with regret. On this day, you have done all that duty and honor required of you, and you have again made me proud."

Nicolas nodded his head in silence. A threshold had been crossed from which he could not turn back. He looked up at the family coat of arms hanging on the wall behind his father.

"Honor. Justice. Mercy."

Nicolas read the words softly. The meaning of the proclamation on the Montferraud coat of arms now made all too real—inscribed in blood by hard experience.

The marquis stared firmly at his son. "Honor first. Honor last. Honor above everything. Now, my young chevalier, you are more than just a servant of glory. Now you understand what it is to be a Montferraud."

Duties of Love, Obligations of Blood

Just two days after Nicolas had been blooded, the marquis let slip over breakfast, that a formal agreement had been reached with the baron allowing Nicolas to begin open courtship of Sérolène. Elated at the apparent success of his father's efforts, Nicolas resolved to spend as much time as he could with the vicomtesse before he sailed for Martinique. He hurried through the remainder of breakfast, donned a light green riding jacket and light chamois riding breeches, then ordered his black stallion saddled so he could pay a call on Sérolène and explore the new boundaries of the open courtship regime.

Riding most of the journey at the gallop, Nicolas arrived at the Salvagnac plantation just before midday, where the steward announced his arrival. The chevalier strode past the vestibule with a confident manner, anticipating the happy sight of the vicomtesse's welcoming countenance. Instead, a stone-faced Baronne de Salvagnac greeted him as he entered *the salon de compagnie*. The baronne reclined at her ease on a pale blue chaise longue. She wore a polonaise gown of very pale yellow, with embroidered petals of red and pink along the skirts. The day was unusually warm and all the windows stood open, but the silk curtains hung limp by the ornately carved woodwork, waiting for the breeze to stir them.

The baronne fanned herself with an elegant Chinese fan made of hand-painted silk. Another visitor sat next to the baronne in the sitting room, whom Nicolas also recognized. "Monsieur le Chevalier d'Argentolle. What a happy surprise."

Nicolas bowed very low, pressing his lips to the baronne's outstretched hand. "Madame de Salvagnac."

The very handsome figure of the Comtesse de Talonge reclined on a chaise longue in perfect indolence, close to the baronne's side. She wore a polonaise of the most delightful shade of pink that Nicolas had ever seen, embroidered with gold oak leaves. Nicolas remembered the comtesse from his brother's ceremony. He bowed in greeting, waiting for the baronne to make the proper introductions.

"Monsieur le Chevalier, I believe you know Madame la Comtesse de Talonge."

Nicolas approached to kiss the outstretched hand of the comtesse. "I had the pleasure of seeing the comtesse at my brother's ceremony, Madame. Madame la Comtesse, I am honored and delighted to see you again. Madame de Blaise speaks of you often, with much admiration and favor."

*

The comtesse inclined her head to acknowledge the compliment, allowing her gaze to wander over Nicolas' pleasing form with a coquettish surfeit of mischief. "Your memory is very good, Monsieur le Chevalier. Please do give my warmest regards to the marquise. Her friendship is so very dear to me, even though its establishment is quite recent. I regret not having been able to stay for supper in celebration of the marriage, especially now that you have reminded me again of just how handsome you are."

Nicolas bowed again to the comtesse. He seemed embarrassed by her praise. She thought the better of him for it.

"You flatter me too much, Madame."

Madame de Talonge shook her head. "On the contrary. I believe I flatter you not at all, Monsieur."

The comtesse motioned for Nicolas to take the seat nearest her. Nicolas sat as directed, though the comtesse sensed his reticence. She suspected he hoped to be released as quickly as possible to go off in search of the real reason for which he had come. She didn't at all blame him for that. She considered it sweet that he had ridden so far and in such haste to see the vicomtesse. And despite his exertions, he didn't at all smell of horse sweat.

"You have come a long way from your estates today, Monsieur. To what do we owe the pleasure of your visit?" the baronne asked, her tone much less playful and indulgent than the comtesse's had been.

The rules of courtship prevented Nicolas from simply stating what everyone knew; that he had rushed out headlong, like any young man in the throes of first love's passion, to see his beloved.

Nicolas cleared his throat. "I decided to take Scipio— the black stallion Monsieur de Salvagnac presented to me— for a run-out. Both of us were in need of a bit of exertion, so I thought I'd ride here to pay my respects and again thank you both for the splendid gift."

Madame de Talonge sat up higher to get a better view of Nicolas' unusual eyes. "You named your horse Scipio? After the Roman Consul?"

"Yes, Madame. I have rather a fondness for the history of Rome. As the horse is jet-black and the consul was also styled *Africanus* in his day, I considered the name fitting."

Madame de Talonge fanned herself in the cloying midday heat, allowing the arc of the painted white paper fan to run along the twin points of her fine powdered bosom. She leaned to the side to admire the sheen on Nicolas' high riding boots, giving the chevalier a healthy eyeful of the rounded mounds of her breasts to admire. She watched his eyes with care, but they never deviated from her own. "Indeed. So you came all the way on horseback and not by carriage, Monsieur?"

"Yes, Madame. I prefer to be in the saddle as long as I can."

The comtesse grinned. "And you do not grow tired from being mounted for so long? Your legs do not ache? You suffer no stiffness in your back?"

"No, Madame. I'm quite used to it, so it doesn't trouble me at all."

It amused the comtesse that the chevalier answered without seeming to be aware of the dual currents of their conversation. She let her gaze wander toward the snug fit of Nicolas' riding breeches, which revealed his superbly muscled thighs to good advantage. Her eyes lingered on the shapely bulge high up on the thigh, too large for the soft fitted leather to wholly conceal.

The comtesse gave Nicolas her best smile. One she normally reserved for her sittings as Venus. "No, it doesn't, does it? How fortunate you are to be so ably endowed."

*

Nicolas might have missed the point of the comtesse pun entirely, but the baronne had not. The baronne saw where the comtesse looked, and she looked too. The comtesse had a point. The chevalier appeared to have more in common with his stallion than a love of hard riding; an added benefit to her niece, should their relationship ever proceed as far as the altar. She might have found it all quite amusing, but for the comtesse's mischievous flirtation.

"Nicolas! Nicolas! I'm so glad to see you!" Éléonore said excitedly, bursting into the room to greet her new brother-in-law.

Nicolas stood at once, grateful for the distraction of his sister-in-law's arrival. "Hello, Elli!"

The baronne beckoned Éléonore to her side. "Aren't you forgetting your manners, Mademoiselle?"

"Oh. Please excuse me, Maman. How do you do, Madame de Talonge?" Éléonore said. She hurried to the comtesse and kissed her on each cheek in apology for greeting Nicolas first.

"Hello my little angel," the comtesse responded with a smile of indulgence.

"Excuse me, Maman, Madame, but may I take Nicolas to hear me practice the harpsichord?" Éléonore asked.

The baronne nodded her consent, eager to have the distraction of Nicolas' presence removed. "If the chevalier would be so inclined, you may go on and take your favorite with you."

"Of course I'd be delighted to hear you play," Nicolas said, no doubt happy as a lark to be freed from the formalities of salon conversation, and hoping to encounter Sérolène on the way to the music room.

Éléonore took Nicolas by the hand as he rose and bowed his courtesies to the baronne and the comtesse. "Would you come with me, please, Monsieur my brother?"

Madame de Talonge watched them depart with avid interest. "My, he *is* delicious, isn't he?"

"Oh, stop it, Charlotte. Haven't your silly games gone far enough?" the baronne snapped.

Madame de Talonge rose from her place and approached her friend, trailing a lazy hand along the length of the baronne's arm and shoulder before allowing it to rest on the soft exposed skin of the baronne's neck. She seemed bemused that the baronne would take her flirtations so ill. The comtesse lay next to the baronne on the chaise longue. She wrapped her arms around the baronne's waist, resting her head on the baronne's full, heaving bosom.

"Come now, my sweet Agnès, there's no need for you to be jealous. You of all people know best the particular preferences of my philosophy. Haven't I given you enough proofs of my sincere devotion?" The comtesse kissed the baronne on top of her bare bosom for emphasis.

The baronne glanced quickly about to make sure they weren't being observed. She shuddered with nervous delight. "Lottie! What if someone should see you?"

The comtesse raised a perfectly manicured brow. "What if they should? What's wrong with me sharing an innocent kiss with my dearest friend?"

The baronne felt her heart quicken with excitement. "I have the other part of the money you asked for."

The comtesse raised both brows in surprise. "So soon? How ever did you manage it?"

The baronne looked down at her hands. "I told my husband I'd lost the money at cards. He got quite upset about it. He even made me promise not to play for such stakes again, but in the end, he gave me what I needed. It's in a heavy strongbox in my chambers. I shall have my servants load it into your coach when you are ready to depart."

The comtesse reached for the baronne's hand, her lips moving higher until they were tantalizingly close to the baronne's own. "You are indeed a wonder, my dear sweet Agnès. You've kept your promise, now I'll keep mine. Come visit me tomorrow at my estate. I shall send everyone away as I promised. And you've no need to bring a large wardrobe, for I assure you, my sweet, your clothes are the last things you shall have need of."

*

Éléonore led Nicolas into the music room. Sérolène sat practicing the harp as he had hoped, looking resplendent in a dark green English styled close bodied gown, with a green and yellow patterned skirt draped over it *à la polonaise*.

"Lena! Look who I've brought to visit!" Éléonore beamed.

Sérolène raised her head from her music, and then broke into a wide grin as she saw the unexpected visitor. "Nicolas! Oh, this is a most delightful surprise! But what are you doing here, and why didn't anyone tell me you had come to call?"

"I arrived not too long ago on horseback. Madame de Salvagnac and the Comtesse de Talonge received me in the *salon de compagnie*. I feared I'd never escape them. Fortunately, Elli came just in time to rescue me, and here I am."

Sérolène took him by the hand, her practice forgotten at once. "Oh, it *is* wonderful to see you. Come, shall we all walk together in your favorite garden?"

Éléonore pouted. "But Nicolas, aren't you going to listen to me play first?"

"Of course, Elli. You go ahead and play and we'll be your audience, all right?" Nicolas agreed.

Satisfied Nicolas had held true to his promise, Éléonore hurried off to the harpsichord. Nicolas stood next to the pianoforte he'd played on his first visit to the Salvagnacs, to listen. He turned to Sérolène to explain. "Will you indulge me, my love? I promised Elli I'd listen to her practice, and I do have her to thank for bringing me here to you."

Sérolène willingly agreed, and they both listened patiently as Éléonore played and then finally exhausted her limited repertoire. After Éléonore had finished, they all then went out to the gardens, Nicolas lending Sérolène his arm and Éléonore his hand as he escorted them around the grounds. As they entered a section ringed on all sides by red and yellow flowers in bloom, Éléonore relinquished her grip on Nicolas to chase a passing butterfly through the hedges.

Sérolène turned toward Nicolas, her gaze curious with amusement. "You seem very pleased about something, Nicolas. Those mischievous dimples tell me so. Would you care to share your secret?"

"I wasn't aware my feelings were so easily transparent," Nicolas said through his grin.

"Perhaps they aren't to others, but they are to me. My love allows me the gift of clairvoyance."

Nicolas laughed aloud. "I suppose it must, my love as you are entirely correct. My happiness stems from a cause important to us both. My father informed me that he had at last come to terms with Monsieur de Salvagnac, who has accepted my request to be allowed to pay you formal court."

Sérolène stared in open-mouthed delight at Nicolas. "Nico! Did you really ask such a thing of my uncle?"

Nicolas nodded, brushing a wandering bee away from the shoulder of his light green coat. "I certainly did, though I admit to being more than a little nervous he might refuse me outright. I am also happy to report I have been allowed the additional privilege of writing to you. I have already sent my first letter by courier, though in my eagerness to see you, I have outdistanced the post."

They laughed together at Nicolas' admission and resumed their walk through the garden. Sérolène turned toward Nicolas, her eyes full of excitement. "Oh, when do you suppose the letter will arrive? And to whom did you entrust the surety of its delivery?"

"Only to my valet Julius, of course. I instructed him to deliver the letter to your uncle first, as had been agreed upon with my father," Nicolas explained.

Sérolène pouted. "To my uncle first? Does this mean it will be lacking in the many sweet phrases and little *tendresses* I've grown so accustomed to hearing in your speech?"

Nicolas leaned close to whisper into her ear. "It is of course more circumspect than I should wish it to be, but by necessity, not by choice. If I were to write to you of everything in my heart, I should be excommunicated at once by your uncle. So I must avail myself of moments such as these to proclaim to you again, and in person, how deeply, truly, and ardently I adore you."

"What about me?" Éléonore chimed in, having arrived back from her game of chase just in time to hear the end of Nicolas' declaration.

"Oh, yes. How could I have neglected you, my dear sister? But you will of course keep our secrets, won't you?" Nicolas asked.

Éléonore nodded her consent with vigor.

"How dearly I love thee, my angel," Nicolas whispered again.

His declaration elicited a pleasing blush and an even more pleasing smile from his beloved. They made several turns through the gardens before Nicolas became aware of the scrutiny of Madame de Salvagnac and the comtesse, who observed them closely through the open doors of the *salon de compagnie, w*hich led directly out into the area of their promenade. Not wishing to overstay his initial welcome, Nicolas thought it prudent to put an early end to his first visit.

The chevalier escorted both Éléonore and Sérolène up the main pathway to take proper leave of his hosts. Nicolas approached the baronne and bowed his farewell. "Thank you for your hospitality, Madame, but I must be on my way now."

Éléonore seemed the most disappointed that the visit musts end so soon. "Maman, can my brother Nicolas come back and visit us again tomorrow?"

The baronne looked from Éléonore to Sérolène. "That is entirely up to him, my dear. But it is a long way from his estate, and you mustn't exhaust him too much with such a request."

"Please, Nicolas, can you come visit us tomorrow? If you do, we can play cards together and you can listen to me sing. If you come early, you can rest here before you ride home, so you won't be so tired." Éléonore pleaded, blissfully unaware of the larger point of Nicolas' visit.

Nicolas smiled at Éléonore's attempt to reason out a solution for him. He glanced quickly at his host to gauge the degree of indulgence at Éléonore's suggestion. "That is very clever of you, Mademoiselle. I shall do my best to try and come."

Éléonore and the baronne both seemed satisfied enough with the response. Nicolas bowed low again, and took his final leave. "Madame de Salvagnac, Madame de Talonge, Mademoiselle de La Bouhaire, Mademoiselle Éléonore."

Before departing for good, Nicolas granted Éléonore the additional favor of a kiss on the cheek, to her very great delight. She went to the foyer with Sérolène to watch Nicolas depart, determined to outdo her *cousine* in waving, as Nicolas mounted his horse. Nicolas turned his mount to wave back at them both, and then rode off.

*

The comtesse watched Sérolène and Éléonore as they bid goodbye to Nicolas from the window, waving until the chevalier disappeared. Sérolène took Éléonore's hand and led her back toward the sitting room. Éléonore looked up at Sérolène, her small brow furrowed in concern. "Do you think my brother will come back tomorrow to see me? Does trying his best mean he will come?"

Sérolène gazed down at Éléonore. She smiled with reassurance. "With any other I might not be so sure, Elli, but if Nicolas say he shall do his best, it means you may very well count it as a certainty."

The comtesse glanced fondly after Éléonore and the vicomtesse, amused by Sérolène's observation. The baronne eyed her with marked interest. She turned her attentions back toward her friend. "She does seem so very much taken with the chevalier."

Madame de Salvagnac began fanning herself vigorously. "She is only a child with a new plaything, Charlotte."

"Not your daughter, dear Agnès, but your niece. How fortunate you are. In light of the chevalier's recent actions and my work on your behalf, his attachment to your Lena will now be looked on with general envy. You are aware also, I trust, that Madame de Blaise and I are now on very cordial terms?"

"I am. We have become friends as well. I heard she regularly attends your salons now."

"Attends? No, my dear, such an innocuous description does not begin to describe the impact she has. Why some weeks ago, just after your rapprochement, she came and held court. Did I not tell you how splendidly she behaved? I do believe she could charm the dead to rise if she wished. You would have been astonished to see how many of her old enemies fell all over themselves to fawn at her feet. By any measure, the visit could be deemed a great success, though I suppose one might wonder at the seemingly unlimited capacity some people have for faultless hypocrisy," the comtesse chuckled.

"We do what we must," the baronne said.

The comtesse heard the sullen tone in the baronne's voice and supposed the arrow of her observation had flown too close to the mark. "Yes we do. And now I have other news which will interest you, dearest. I have heard the Marquis de Blaise plans to add the seigneuries of Cerneaux and Blinfey to the chevalier's domains. That young man's income will more than double to over half a million livres[viii] a year. The information came to me from the marquise herself. I also had it corroborated by a very reliable source."

The baronne turned to stare. "Half a million livres! It's an enormous sum. Are you certain it's true?"

The comtesse sipped from her glass of sweetened Jerez, a treat she always allowed herself in the early afternoon. "You may rely upon what I have disclosed as being accurate. You know that reptile Noirmince-Vauginon, Baron de Ginestas?"

"Only by reputation, Lottie, though I believe my husband has had dealings with him in relation to my late brother's will."

"How interesting," the comtesse said, filing away the information for later use. "Ginestas has very high-level contacts in the office of the Keeper of the Seals. I managed to pry the information out of him when he last visited my salon."

"In exchange for what?" the baronne asked.

"He asked me about the true size of the Comtesse de Marbéville's dowry, and if dowries of comparable natures would be provided to the other eligible ladies of your household," the comtesse replied without guile or hesitation.

The baronne's gaze shifted with unease. "And what did you say?"

The comtesse finished her *Jerez* in one long draught, setting the glass down on the table beside her. A lackey instantly appeared to refill it. "I told him I could not speak for you or Monsieur de Salvagnac, but I supposed Julienne's dowry to be gargantuan and saw no reason to presume the eventual dowries of your daughter and niece would be otherwise."

The comtesse took another sip from her glass. "But enough talk of him and all the rest like him. I detest them all! Corrupt, dried-up old men with expensive tastes and grand titles, but not nearly enough money to support their manner of living. They will stoop to anything to fill their coffers, swarming after the dowries of your children like vultures. You, dear Agnès, are so fortunate to have a suitor for your niece who brings a considerable fortune of his own to any alliance. With the wealth his domains already produce, I wager the chevalier wouldn't care if his bride came with a dowry at all."

The baronne considered what the comtesse had revealed. The more she discovered of Nicolas' great wealth, the more she became inclined to see his good qualities over the bad. "Do you think it's safe for him to attempt the journey back to his estate so late in the day? Perhaps I should send men along with him to ensure his safety."

The comtesse laughed. "Concerned about your investment, are you? You needn't worry, I think. In light of what he did to Petitfleur and his men, I doubt many would dare to challenge him."

"What do you mean?" the baronne asked.

The comtesse perked up to find that she possessed knowledge of import that the baronne lacked. It gave her a sense of both validation and power. "Have you not heard? The drunken beast took a party of his slave hunters in pursuit of some runaways. There were five of them in all—his eldest son Michel, an overseer, and two trackers. Apparently, they made the mistake of taking a shortcut across the marquis' lands. Michel almost collided with the chevalier, who had been riding through the countryside with the marquis. Young Petitfleur fell from his horse and badly injured himself. I'm told his arm is now hideously deformed as a result and he can no longer use it."

"My word! How unfortunate for him and his future prospects," the baronne said with sympathy.

"That, my dear, is the least of his misfortunes now. The elder Petitfleur always had a knack for finding trouble and then compounding it upon himself. Rumor has it, that he and his men committed the abomination upon the blacks found last month not far from the Blaise estate. Mayhap his arrogance in escaping the justice he deserved made him careless. This time, however, he went too far. He made the grave error of insulting the chevalier to his face, accusing him of causing the fall and the injury to his son. Of course the chevalier answered back most hotly, trading insult for insult."

"Did Petitfleur not realize by the comportment and dress of the chevalier that he erred most grievously?"

"Apparently not. Instead, he became incensed, then made the fatal mistake of ordering his men to attack the chevalier. But Petitfleur soon discovered d'Argentolle very different from the shackled, half-starved human prey he liked to chase."

The baronne sat up with interest. "What happened? Was there more than just a quarrel? The boy didn't seem to have been perturbed in the least!"

The comtesse took a long sip from her glass. "Three men dead in the blink of an eye and Petitfleur minus his head."

The baronne's expression betrayed her astonishment. "Dear God! To think he did all that and has not a scratch upon him. But is there to be no official inquiry into what occurred?"

"Everyone considered Petitfleur vermin and a roundly detested nuisance. I imagine just his family will mourn him, and then only briefly, since as a result of his actions they are now bankrupt. Besides, who would contest the word of the marquis, or of the chevalier, for that matter? This latest incident will only add to the luster of the young man's glory. He'll be a saint to the women victimized by Petitfleur's foul habits, and a hero to the slaves who had grown to fear the ruthlessness of Petitfleur's men. I presumed you already knew of all this when you received him earlier. If I were you, Agnès, I should do everything possible to encourage his attachment to your niece, given his character, fame, fortune, and the fact that he completely adores her."

The baronne searched the comtesse's eyes for any hint of exaggeration or deception. "Do you really think so? How can you be sure he truly loves her as you say?"

Madame de Talonge smiled provocatively at her most intimate of friends. "I consider myself something of an expert when it comes to adoration, and in this case, I've no doubt he's wholly besotted. Why I all but threw myself at him when he arrived and he scarce paid any attention to me at all. He seemed so pleased when Éléonore came to rescue him I almost laughed."

"So you were just testing him?" the baronne said.

"Of course, kitten. That young man has eyes only for his vicomtesse. Why he didn't even try to sneak a peek at my bosom, when I all but waved it in his face. I needed to be sure of his faithfulness, and now I am. You should be sure of it too. Now give me your kisses. I fear I must take my leave as well. I wish to be sure all is ready to receive you."

The baronne obliged, pressing her lips to each cheek, as Madame de Salvagnac rose to see the comtesse off.

As soon as the comtesse had gone, the baronne rang a bell to summon her maid, Maria. "I shall be taking a trip tomorrow and will be away at least a week. You may start preparing my things for the journey."

Maria curtsied in understanding. "Will Madame be going out, or staying indoors?"

The baronne went to the window to watch the comtesse's coach pass through the gate of the outer courtyard. "I shall need only a few dresses, but double the number of nightgowns. With all this humid weather as of late, I shall wish to sleep in as much comfort as I can."

*

Nicolas reached the outskirts of his father's lands with just a few hours of daylight remaining. He slowed the black stallion Scipio as he rode across the slight rise at the top of the long meadow, not far from where the incident with Petitfleur and his men had occurred. An equerry put a new horse through its paces in the field to his left. Off to the right, he spied a coach along the road in the distance, which looked to have broken a wheel in a rut. Nicolas brought Scipio to a halt and withdrew his spyglass. The driver and footman attempted to repair the carriage. A single lady passenger watched by the side of the road while they worked.

Nicolas turned toward the field to his left and waved to the equerry to attract his attention. The man seemed to recognize the great black horse and its rider at once. He guided his mount toward the road and hurried to reach the chevalier. The equerry removed his hat and bowed from the saddle as he reached Nicolas' side. "Monseigneur, how may I be of service?"

"Bring some men and help them repair the coach there, and then fetch my carriage to pick up the lady who has been stranded. We'll take her back to the estate until the repairs are completed. I suppose the men will be hungry from their labors, so see to some food and drink for them as well."

The equerry nodded and rode off at once to carry out Nicolas' orders. Nicolas urged Scipio forward toward the coach, covering the remaining distance at the walk. It took him only a short time to reach the stranded vehicle.

The driver eyed Nicolas as he approached. He removed his hat and bowed low in respectful greeting. "Good day, Monsieur."

"Good day to you as well," Nicolas offered back. "A broken wheel, I take it?"

"Yes, Monsieur. These old eyes aren't what they once were, I suppose. I should have seen that rut back there."

"Help will be along soon enough. I've sent for some men to come and speed your repair. I also took the liberty of sending for my carriage. Any passengers you have are welcome to wait at my family's estate until you should be ready to resume your journey."

The driver bowed very low in appreciation. "I thank you again, Monsieur. May I ask how I am to address you?"

"You may address me as Monsieur le Chevalier d'Argentolle."

At the announcement of Nicolas' rank, the driver took off his hat and held it in his hands. "Albert Agouti at your service, Monsieur le Chevalier. How fortuitous our small calamity has turned out to be."

"How so?" Nicolas asked.

"We carry but one passenger, and she journeyed to visit a gentleman of the same appellation you lay claim to. We were not quite sure of the road to follow to your estate and decided on this one. If our wheel had not come off, we'd have likely passed it by."

Nicolas wondered who had come to visit him. He hadn't recognized the lady he had seen through his spyglass. "Where is your guest now, might I ask?"

The driver pointed to a large tree about a hundred yards away. "Madame walked over there to take shade while we work."

Nicolas shifted in the saddle as he heard the sound of his carriage and drivers approaching. "Here are my men now. They'll have brought water for you and some cakes and pies as well, in case you are hungry. I'll bid you good day now. I shall go and see about our guest."

The driver doffed his hat as Nicolas rode toward the stranded coach's passenger. The coachman joined Agouti, resting his back against the broken wheel they were trying to repair, which had been propped up against a nearby tree.

The coachman nodded his head toward Nicolas. "Now there goes a proper gentleman, Albert. If all the seigneurs were as considerate as he is, France wouldn't be as deep in the shit as we are now."

Further down the road, Nicolas arrived at the large shade tree. He dismounted as the coach's passenger emerged from partial concealment on the other side of the trunk. Nicolas studied the lady's face as he moved forward to introduce himself, finding it vaguely familiar, though he knew he had not met her before. The fullness of middle-age sat pressed upon the lady's shoulders like an invisible weight. She had overdressed for the heat and the season and had begun to perspire. The clothes she wore belonged to another, earlier era, and had the faded quality of things whose best years had passed. Nicolas had the impression that the lady had reached deep into her wardrobe to select the finest garments she had, regardless of their lack of currency or style. As Nicolas approached more closely, he saw that even the fabric at the hem of her skirts had worn and faded with age.

The lady watched him with care as he approached. She seemed nervous, with very fair skin which had already begun to color from the day's strong sunlight. A gentle breeze tugged at the wide flat brim of her hat. She kept it in place with one hand, and with the other, fought a holding action against the stray wisps of reddish hair that dropped from beneath the brim to cascade down onto her forehead.

Nicolas dismounted, removed his hat and bowed low. He placed his left hand on the hilt of his sword to prevent it from dragging on the ground as he performed the ritual of courtesy. "Madame. Please allow me to introduce myself. I am Nicolas de Montferraud, Chevalier d'Argentolle. I understand from your driver that your coach became stranded while you were on your way to see me. Will you allow me to offer you a ride to our estate in my carriage? It's not far off and you may wait there in comfort for your coach to be repaired."

The lady returned his bow with a graceful curtsey, a touch of sadness clouding her smile. Nicolas knew then where he had seen the face before, and guessed at her identity.

"Thank you, Monsieur. That is very kind of you."

She hesitated a moment before accepting his proffered arm, then allowed herself to be led back toward the approaching Montferraud carriage, an open cabriolet. Nicolas helped the lady to her seat, then nodded to one of the footmen, who approached hurriedly to receive his instructions. "Take Scipio back to the château and see to it the men have all they need to finish the repairs."

As the man nodded and led the great black horse away, Scipio swiped his head at Nicolas, annoyed at his swift abandonment. Nicolas ducked the blow, laughing as he moved forward to stroke the horse's neck and ears. He kissed the stallion upon the nose in apology. "All right, I know you are cross with me, and I shall make it up to you with a good ride tomorrow. Your gentle Aemilia waits to welcome you home. Go and spend the remaining energy you have with her."

Nicolas patted Scipio on the shoulder as the groom led the horse away, admiring the powerful gait of the magnificent stallion. Nicolas then mounted the carriage and sat opposite his guest and closer to the driver. He would ride backward as the carriage moved forward. "To the château, if you please."

A moment later, they were on their way. Nicolas nodded to the footman, who rode on the footboard at the back of the open carriage. The man opened a parasol over the lady to shade her from the afternoon sun.

"Well, Madame Petitfleur, to what do I owe the honor of your visit? I must confess it is a surprise…though I assure you it is not unwelcome."

The lady looked up in surprise. "You know who I am, Monsieur?"

"There is much of you in your son's face, Madame. I confess I have thought of him often since that terrible day."

Madame Petitfleur wrung her hands with relief. "Ah, Monsieur, you do not know how much I am gratified to hear it. I had feared to introduce myself to you earlier out of concern you might not receive me if I revealed my identity to you. I see now my apprehensions were foolish and unwarranted."

Nicolas leaned slightly forward so that he could hear his guest over the sound of the moving carriage. "May I ask, Madame, how you and your family have been faring? I wish you to know I did not desire to…to take anyone's life, and I have much regretted that things came to pass the way they did."

Madame Petitfleur wiped at her eyes. Nicolas relinquished his kerchief to his guest. It took several moments for her to compose herself. Nicolas turned politely away to admire the passing scenery, allowing Madame Petitfleur a moment to retrieve her emotions.

Madame Petitfleur cleared her throat and attempted a brave smile. "Thank you, Monsieur, for this kerchief and your kind words. My husband never had temperance in him, neither in speech nor in manners. Rough and hard, that's what he was, like the land he toiled, I suppose. I always worried his temper would bring him to grief one day… and so it has at last. You asked about my family, Monsieur. That is the reason for my visit today. I come to you on bended knee, a complete and utter supplicant. By the fault of my husband's hard and impulsive life, and the circumstance of his unexpected death, we have now been utterly ruined."

Nicolas leaned forward again, his concern clear and sincere upon his face. "But how did this all come to be? I implore you, Madame, to tell me everything."

Madame Petitfleur brought the handkerchief to her cheeks again, as she began to recount all the misfortunes that had befallen her family. "We left Martinique last year in some haste, after selling our plantation there. I discovered only after my husband's death that the reason for our swift flight involved enormous debts still owed to his many creditors for taxes and seeds. Upon his death, the creditors confiscated the plantation here to settle those obligations, along with all the other assets of our household they could lay claim to. In the end, we are left with little more than the clothes on our backs and some few personal belongings. After we were forced from our home, my children and I found temporary shelter with the nuns in Cap François. I had hoped perhaps to return to France and start anew, but we don't even have enough money for food, let alone passage back to France."

"You wish to return to France, Madame?"

Madame Petitfleur sighed, her shoulders hunched forward by the weight of the accumulated misfortune she had been forced to bear all her life. "What else can we do, Monsieur? I have three young daughters and a son just seventeen, who has now been crippled as a result of his fall and cannot work. I had some talent in my youth as a seamstress, but I gave it up when I married my husband. If I had enough to open a small shop, I should at least be able to support my family. My parents are long dead, you see…and so are my husband's."

The carriage passed through the outer gate and into the outer courtyard of the Montferraud estate. Madame Petitfleur marveled at the size and splendor of the Blaise château. Nicolas nodded his head in understanding. "I see, Madame. Rest assured I shall do what I can to assist you."

Madame Petitfleur lifted her gaze toward Nicolas as a penitent might look up toward heaven. "Bless you, Monsieur!"

The grooms helped Madame Petitfleur to dismount and then escorted her to the front of the receiving salon. Nicolas stood apart by the entranceway. "Will you excuse me for a few moments, Madame? I need to make arrangements with regard to your situation. If you need anything, just ring the bell and someone will attend to you with promptness."

The chevalier motioned for one of the two grooms to escort his guest to a seat and see to her comfort. A servant led Madame Petitfleur to a comfortable sofa. Moments later, another servant brought a pitcher of lemon juice and water sweetened with sugar, along with several pastries and small cakes on a large silver tray. The lackey poured Madame Petitfleur a glass and then retired to the edge of the room, as Madame Tarnaut helped herself to the refreshments.

After several minutes, Nicolas returned, bearing a sealed letter in one hand and a large purse in the other. Nicolas handed the letter to Madame Petitfleur. The envelope bore just a single name written prominently across the front. "The contents of this letter should see to the longer-term needs of your family, Madame. This purse should take care of any pressing needs you might have, including a return to France if that is what you wish. The letter is for a Monsieur Valduringe. He handles some of our banking affairs and has an office in Port-au-Prince. I shall write to him to expect you and the letter you carry. Please ensure the letter remains sealed, lest he think it tampered with and refuse to accept its contents as genuine. I regret to burden you with these details, but it is the custom of our transactions together."

Madame Petitfleur reached out and took Nicolas' hands. She pressed them to her lips in thanks. "No, Madame. Such gratitude as you display is not necessary. I do only what I must. What honor and justice compel me to do."

The lackey at the door approached Nicolas to deliver a whispered message. Nicolas nodded and turned to face his guest. "Your repaired coach awaits you, Madame. Remember to see Monsieur Valduringe as soon as you can."

Madame Petitfleur rose and curtsied low. "We are forever in your debt, Monsieur."

Nicolas shook his head. "Madame, there are but two things I must ask of you. I ask your word that you will not use any of the money I have given you to purchase or enslave another human being. I ask also that you not tell your children what I have done on your behalf. I do not wish them to feel indebted to me in any way, after the loss I have caused them."

Madame Petitfleur nodded her agreement. "You have my solemn oath, Monsieur, on behalf of myself and all my family."

Nicolas bowed his acceptance and escorted Madame Petitfleur to the waiting carriage. As he watched it depart, he felt as if part of the burden of the lives he had taken had been lifted from him. He turned and went inside in search of his mother, to share with her all the interesting events of the day.

*

Madame Petitfleur opened the pouch she had been given and counted the gold coins in astonishment. The chevalier had given her at least five thousand livres, enough to buy passage to France and start a seamstress shop of her own, and perhaps even open a small inn or tavern as well. She felt relief beyond imagining. Now she could begin again and on her own terms. Her son would have a living and her daughters, dowries.

Madame Petitfleur kissed the letter bearing Nicolas' signature and mouthed a quick prayer of thanks. "Heaven bless you, Monsieur. You have helped those who had the least right to expect it of you."

She lowered her head in prayer. "Dear Lord, look after the chevalier as he has looked after us. I pray you always keep him safe and secure."

*

Nicolas rose early the next morning to take breakfast before setting out to cover the almost twenty miles to the Salvagnac plantation on horseback again. He decided to again trade the comfort of a coach for the speed and pleasure of riding, and to keep his promise to Scipio to give him another long run out.

When he arrived at the Salvagnac estate, the steward François ushered him again into the main salon, but this time, he waited but a few minutes and before being happily surprised when Sérolène herself came to greet him, accompanied by her governess. Because his parole had been given to vouchsafe his conduct, Nicolas socialized freely with the vicomtesse, without the strict scrutiny which normally governed the relationships of post-pubescent and unmarried young ladies. The chevalier stayed almost the entire day, riding back home in the late afternoon and racing against the twilight.

For more than a week, Nicolas visited Sérolène every day, despite the length of the ride. The baronne had gone to visit the comtesse for an extended stay, and the baron had often already gone to town to tend to his various affairs before Nicolas arrived. In his absence, Nicolas and Sérolène passed the hours under the eye of Madame Tarnaut, with Éléonore as a constant companion. Planted in such fruitful soil, the roots of love and friendship grew deep and intertwined.

*

On the eighth of January, Nicolas left his estate at dawn in order to spend as much time with Sérolène as possible. He arrived in the early morning but Sérolène anticipated his coming and sat waiting for him in the main parlor. They made good use of their autonomy and spent the entire day together—playing at cards, singing in the music room, acting out plays or walking through the gardens, invariably in the company of Éléonore, or sometimes Madame Tarnaut, who regulated them loosely from a distance.

As late afternoon approached, Nicolas strolled in the garden, arm in arm with Sérolène. He had news to tell her. News he had waited until the end of the day to reveal. "I'm to depart for Martinique tomorrow. I'm not sure when I shall return, my love. My father is sending me away to begin my preparations for the École Militaire. I regret to say it, but today will be my last visit for some time."

The look in Sérolène's eyes made his regret at leaving all the more poignant. "I'm sorry, my dearest. I presumed I would have more time here with you before I departed, but one of our ships has arrived in port earlier than expected, and my father wishes me to embark upon it tomorrow. You must know how desperately I shall miss you. Perhaps I should have told you earlier, but I didn't have the heart to mention it and spoil our last day together."

Sérolène gazed with longing at Nicolas. "Will you promise to write to me often?"

"Every day, my love."

"I should very much like that, Nico, but how will you be able to deliver your letters? My uncle will never allow so many to reach me."

"François has promised he will be my go-between," Nicolas revealed.

"Truly? That's wonderful, and kind of him to do so." Sérolène said.

"We are fortunate to have found an ally among your father's men. I'm happy your servants seem to trust me. There is a daily mail ship between the islands. My valet Julius will carry my private letters to the port and deliver them to François when he undertakes his daily errands for

Monsieur de Salvagnac. François is willing to transmit my private letters to you, as well as receive your private letters for me. I shall continue to write to you by the normal means so suspicions aren't aroused, but we shall also have our secret post, in which we may speak with more openness to each other."

Sérolène lifted her head at the approach of her governess. "I suppose it's at least some consolation. It seems Madame Tarnaut wishes to speak with me."

Madame Tarnaut motioned toward Sérolène to come inside, eyeing Nicolas with sympathy. "Mademoiselle, have you forgotten that your lessons are today? Your music teacher has arrived. You must come along presently to begin your lessons."

Sérolène sighed and hung her head. Apparently, she had indeed forgotten. "Please tell Monsieur Barthélemy to wait in the music room. I shall be on my way as soon as I see the chevalier off, Madame."

Madame Tarnaut shook her head, but indulged her charge nonetheless. Nicolas knew the Salvagnac household held him in high esteem, and would do nearly anything for him. They felt the same way about the vicomtesse.

"Oh, why must my lessons be today of all days, when I'm to have my last glimpse of you for who knows how long? I insist on accompanying you to the stables to see you safely to your horse," Sérolène said with a pout.

*

Nicolas passed through the garden with Sérolène, taking a path alongside the western promenade that led to the courtyard and stables. As they turned toward the large stone building, Nicolas felt as if he should at least say something to occupy the silence with more than bitter regret. "Are you sure you desire to proceed with me all the way, my love? A stable is fraught with many inconveniences which might prove very troublesome to a lady."

"You know more about such things than I do, I'm sure, but nothing will dissuade me from staying with you until the last possible moment. Besides, I convinced Uncle long ago to allow me to learn how to ride, so I am not completely unfamiliar with horses and their upkeep. I may not be the horseman you are, but I can make my way with a fair degree of proficiency. Perhaps when you return we can ride together?" Sérolène suggested.

Nicolas glanced at Sérolène with newfound appreciation. "You can ride! Why didn't you tell me? This is splendid news. I very much look forward to our riding together. You can take Aemilia, she's as gentle as a fawn and will carry you with no trouble at all."

They reached the stable doors, the grooms and equerries raised their eyes in surprise and their hats in respect to the vicomtesse. Sérolène ignored the curiosity of the stablemen. As a lady of the house, she could do and go as she pleased. "In which stall is Monsieur d'Argentolle's horse being kept? I wish to inspect the suitability of its accommodations for myself."

One of the men bowed and led the way into the large stone horse stable. "This way, Mademoiselle, Monseigneur."

Sérolène walked behind Nicolas, who did his best to clear a path free of fresh manure and other leavings.

Sérolène held her nose at the smell. "Nico, it smells so awful!"

She began to giggle, perhaps doubting the wisdom of being so adventurous. The further they went into the barn, the stronger the odor of dung, horse, and human sweat became. They reached the last stall where the stallion Scipio had been placed to keep him away from the other horses and far away from the grooms. The great black horse made quite a noise, prancing and pawing the ground. The groom stopped several feet away from the stallion's stall.

The stallion snorted his irritation, having caught scent of his master, and eager to be on his way. Nicolas turned to the wary groom. "Go and bring my equipage. I'll walk him out and saddle him myself. He's touchy around strangers. I wouldn't want you to get a kick in the head."

"Aye, Monseigneur, I know well enough what the brute can do. I got too close to him after feeding and he nearly took my head off with a kick," the groom related bowing in compliance, as he set off at once to fetch the equipment and escape the devil horse.

Nicolas opened the door to the stall and entered with caution, his senses alert until satisfied that Scipio's temper had not been aroused. He took the horse's bridle and stroked him on the nose, preparing to lead him out. The stallion snorted and sniffed, turning his head to the side to get a better look at Sérolène.

"Come, my dearest, I think he wants to say hello to you."

Sérolène held back, unsure whether she should accept the stallion's invitation. "It's all right, I promise you."

Nicolas extended his hand to Sérolène. The vicomtesse grasped it firmly and joined him in the stall.

"Go ahead, pet him on the nose, like this." Nicolas showed her how to do it.

Sérolène reached out tentatively, stroking Scipio very lightly.

"Be firm my love. He's a big brute. He needs to feel the surety of your touch."

Sérolène pressed harder and the stallion rewarded her by lifting his head to lick her hand. It made Sérolène laugh with delight. Nicolas grinned. "You see, he likes you. He's a clever horse and quite particular, but it seems he has taken a fancy to you already. Perhaps he'll even let you ride him one day."

"Do you really think he might?"

"It's very possible. He's not usually so free with his kisses."

Sérolène pressed herself close to Nicolas, their intimacy hidden by the walls of the stall and the height of the large stallion. "Neither am I, Monsieur. But I do make exceptions."

Nicolas lifted a watchful eye toward the front of the stables. "Séro…the grooms."

"They won't come back here with Scipio's stall door open. Everyone but you is afraid of that horse. Besides, Nico, I'm fifteen today and this may be our last moment together for some time. I need my fill of your kisses now to sustain me while you are gone."

Nicolas looked at Sérolène in surprise then held her very close. "Today is your birthday? I'm sorry, my love, I didn't know. How cruel it now seems to leave you on this day. I promise I shall make it up to you, though."

"Your kiss will be gift enough," Sérolène urged. She pressed her lips against his mouth, pried his lips open with her tongue, and drew forth the very breath from his lungs.

Nicolas held Scipio's bridle in his left hand as the stallion snorted his displeasure at being ignored so thoroughly. After a time, the sharp jerk of the rein warned Nicolas they had already been alone together in the stables longer than the rules of propriety deemed suitable.

Nicolas broke their kiss with reluctance, then drew Sérolène close so he could bestow his cross of kisses in parting. "Happy birthday, my love. Come, let's walk him out."

Once outside, Sérolène shielded herself behind her parasol to prevent the scrutiny of others as the groom carried forward Scipio's blanket and saddle. Nicolas placed the saddle blanket across the stallion's back and saddled Scipio himself. He checked and rechecked the cinches, fittings, and strap, then made ready to mount up. He adjusted his sword on his hip for riding, then turned to take his leave of Sérolène. Seeing her eyes well with tears, he couldn't bring himself to say a final farewell.

"May Scipio and I walk you back to the house?"

Sérolène nodded, and took his arm. As they walked, Nicolas filled her ears with endearments and her heart with love, reminding her of his promise to write and assuring her he would return as soon as he could. They stopped in front of the entrance to the château. Nicolas could delay no more.

He took Sérolène's hand and squeezed it tenderly. "Madame Tarnaut will be cross with you if she sees your tears. Will you play me a pretty tune to send me on my way? And tell Elli I'll miss her too?"

Sérolène nodded, as Nicolas mounted his horse.

"Au revoir, my angel," Nicolas said, his voice thick with emotion.

Sérolène gave Nicolas a brave but melancholy smile. "Au revoir, my eternal love."

Nicolas blew Sérolène a final kiss, then turned his mount and rode briskly away. He dared not look over his shoulder, because if he did he would turn around and ride straight back. And as much as he wished to stay, Nicolas knew that for a Montferraud, obligations of blood always took precedence over duties of love.

The Dirk and the Sword

Malveau looked at the cards staring face up in front of him. Another rotten hand in a streak of luckless draws. "Damn your eyes, Lacombe, you've won three in a row. Fate seems unusually kind to you this night."

The seaman Lacombe reached out to claim his winnings, grinning as he scooped the pile of coins into his purse. "You know how it is, gents. Lady Luck is a fickle mistress. But don't lose faith; she may take up your cause again tomorrow."

The tanner Pandini threw his luckless cards onto the table with a scowl. "Perhaps it's fate, perhaps something else."

Pandini looked toward Malveau to see if he would take up the implied challenge. He had lost a month of wages tonight, and he wouldn't mind winning them back in a fight, fair or not. The winner, Lacombe, looked tough but not insurmountable. Pandini would need help. Malveau seemed just the sort of fellow to do the business. He had the air of a hungry wolf and the looks to match, handsome, but in a swarthy kind of manner, which reeked of hidden villainy—the kind of man to have about in a scrap. Malveau, however, seemed unconcerned about his mounting losses. Instead, he motioned to the serving wench to fetch another flagon of drink. Pandini shrugged, wishing he were the kind of man with money to throw away, or better yet, with luck to win at cards.

Malveau turned toward the tanner with a half-smile. "Come now, Pandini, have another glass of rum and wash away your sulk. A gambler's life ebbs and flows like the tides. Lacombe seems an honest fellow. I'm sure he's not the sort to try and cheat anyone."

*

Lacombe nodded at the open vote of support. For a moment, it seemed as if there might be trouble, but Malveau seemed to be a gentleman, at least about losing. Lacombe secured his purse inside his coat pocket then finished the last of his rum. He had a big day on the morrow and didn't need an advance of trouble to spoil it. Pandini looked a quarrelsome sort of fellow. In any case, best to go while the run of luck still sat with him.

Lacombe pushed his chair back from the table. "Very gentlemanly of you, Malveau, but I've had my fill of this place. I think I'll have a last drink at a proper tavern. Why don't *you* come join me? We'll raise a glass to good fortune and I'll buy you a treat of some decent wine."

Malveau dropped a few coins on the uneven surface of wood then winked at the surly tanner. He stood, preparing to go with the seaman Lacombe, leaving Pandini to finish his drink alone. "I'd be delighted to, Monsieur Lacombe, and I know the perfect place for it. Marseilles can be a dangerous city, my friend. Please allow me the honor of escorting you to a favorite watering hole of mine. It's not far from here. Quite near the docks, actually. You might even be able to see your ship from there. What did you say its name was again?"

Lacombe swayed to his feet, adjusting his black seaman's bicorne with care before leaving a single coin on the table for the serving wench. "The *Belle Héloïse*."

Lacombe oriented himself in the general direction of the tavern's front door, and exited with Malveau into the dark but still bustling streets of the port. The two companions dissolved into the crowd, linked only by vice and convenience. Malveau grabbed a torch from a nearby wall sconce and held it aloft to provide light as they walked.

The puffed up hangover of a good night at the gambling table made Lacombe giddy and talkative. He patted his coat to make sure he hadn't lost his papers. "I haven't seen the ship yet, but I'm to be the new purser on board. I have my orders right here. We're off to St. Domingue to escort a bunch of aristos back to France. A boatload of high lords and ladies, so I'm told. The officers' share of the cargo ought to be worth a pretty penny, and there's plenty of skirt to get up and under in the colonies—light meat and dark—whatever suits a man's fancy."

Lacombe grinned as he reflected on the bright nature of his future prospects. He loosened his collar against the oppressive Marseilles heat, then took off his coat and slung it over his shoulder, hoping the faint stirring of a late night breeze would help clear his head of the fog of too much drink.

"Nothing quite like those Creole wenches to keep a man's candle lit, eh?" Malveau said.

Lacombe grinned wide. "Lit and properly waxed. And with my winnings tonight friend, I'll be able to grease the wick as often as I like!"

The crowds had thinned out in the area they walked through, but Lacombe took no real notice. A stray glob of spittle clung to Lacombe's lower lip. Lacombe sensed it and wiped his mouth on the sleeve of his coat.

Malveau lowered the torch in his hand to shin level as they walked. He put an arm around Lacombe's shoulder. Lacombe flinched at the unexpected contact, but then relaxed as he looked at Malveau's broad grin. "It seems you've led an adventuresome life, my friend. Tell me about your ship and crew, and the other ships you've sailed on, Monsieur Lacombe."

Lacombe liked being called Monsieur. Malveau had good manners and seemed more than friendly. What could be the harm in chatting about his experiences? He gave Malveau a good earful of his exploits and adventures in detail, until the irresistible call of nature brought his narrative to a necessary halt.

"Hold on a sec. I've gotta piss," Lacombe said.

Malveau stepped back. Lacombe unbuttoned his breeches and urinated against a nearby wall. He stared into the gloom to his right and left, trying to take his bearings, but couldn't make out any visible points of reference. "Damn me for a suckling babe. My head's beatin' like a drum and we've walked down a blind alley haven't we?"

Malveau didn't reply. The torch suddenly went out. Lacombe stood holding his limp penis in hand, waiting for his eyes to adjust to the abrupt transition to blackness. A cloud passed across the face of the half moon. The air smelled thick with the scent of the sea. He heard the sound of nearby waves lapping against the beach.

Lacombe shook his head. "I think you're lost, Malveau. We're near the waterfront. I can hear the waves rolling in on the beach. Maybe I'd best pass on the drink. I have a big day tomorrow. Perhaps I'd do better with some sleep."

Malveau swung the dead torch in his hands with both hands, striking Lacombe across the side of the head.

"No, I'm not lost, my drunk fool of a friend, but it seems you are!"

Malveau stared down at Lacombe's fallen body. The right side of Lacombe's skull showed a fist-sized dent where the torch had struck. Blood oozed out onto the dark cobblestones as the body quivered reflexively in death. Malveau had killed before. He knew better than to waste time gawking at the body. He removed the fat purse of winnings from the dead man's jacket and stripped the body, careful to avoid getting blood on the garments he took.

With darkness as an ally, Malveau quickly changed into the dead seaman's coat, shirt, boots, and hat. He took Lacombe's identity papers and stuffed them into the inside pocket of his new jacket. With a quick glance around to make sure the area remained clear of any other souls, he then began dragging Lacombe's body toward the nearby shoreline. Several ship launches had been hauled up onto the beach and tied to posts along the shore. Malveau heaved Lacombe's body into the first launch he came across and wrapped it up in the boat's small canvas sail. He loaded the macabre cocoon down with stones and then secured it with bits of rope from the launch, then pulled the launch into the sea and hopped aboard. It took him less than an hour to row out into the middle of the harbor under the cover of darkness and dump the body. As he rowed back to shore, he laughed to himself at the naïveté of his victim.

"Did you really think I'd let you make off with a fat purse of my money?"

Malveau spat into the water, an offering to the demons of the night who watched over him. He almost regretted killing the poor bastard, but the police had trailed him to the city and he needed to find a way out of Marseilles and fast. Passage on Lacombe's ship seemed the perfect way to do it.

Lacombe had told him that the crew didn't know him yet. No reason to believe they wouldn't accept him in Lacombe's place. And he had enough real experience on slavers and cattle ships to pull it off. Besides, how could he resist the temptation of so many rich and noble lords all together in one place—the men for the robbing, and the women for the taking?

Malveau grinned. Despite the odds, once again his luck had held. He had a new identity, orders of passage, and a purse full of money. Soon he'd be on his way to the colonies where the law wouldn't be able to find him. If he played his cards right, Lucifer, whom he regarded as his own patron saint, would find many new dark and profitable adventures for him to undertake.

*

"You're late, Monsieur Lacombe."

The voice belonged to Capitaine Philippe Closon, and it betrayed his irritation as he addressed the last of his officers to report for duty aboard his ship, the *Belle Héloïse*. To the captain, tardiness equaled sloth. Both were willful faults he would not tolerate among his crew or his officers.

Closon looked all of his almost fifty years, more than thirty-five of which had been spent at sea. His skin bore the marks of his chosen profession, its surface as hardy and weathered as the canvas the crew hauled overhead. After a lifetime of sailing, his compact frame had been made wiry and tough, like the great coils of rope holding his sails in place. His eyes had the color of the ocean, dark blue and brooding, anchored in a weather-beaten face, which might have easily found a place upon a ship's masthead. Closon always wore a uniform of black when he sailed, with gold epaulets to denote his rank, but no other form of decoration.

Only his bicorne hat kept the record of his many years at sea, adorned on both sides with copious gold braiding, white feather trim along the crest and a large white ostrich plume on the left side. He stared down the late arrival, waiting to bite off the newcomer's excuses should he be foolish enough to offer any.

The junior officer began to explain himself. "Yes, Mon Capitaine. Sorry, Mon Capitaine. I had some trouble finding the correct pier…"

Closon raised hand cut off any more justifications. He sat behind his desk in the captain's stateroom, glancing down at the newcomer's papers, which lay open before him. Though Bernard Lacombe's record of service appeared spotless, he had never served with Closon before, nor any of the other officers and crew.

"If I want explanations or excuses, I'll ask for them. Understood?"

"Yes, Mon Capitaine!" Lacombe replied smartly.

Closon scrutinized the man in front of him with a puzzled glance. For the third time he'd addressed him like a landlubber. Closon wanted to know why. "I learned my trade in the French Navy, before I became a merchant captain. In the navy we have a saying, Monsieur Lacombe, there is *mon Dieu* and *mon cul*, but never *mon capitaine.*"[ix]

The newcomer turned pale. Perhaps nerves had gotten the best of him? If he weren't short staffed with a tight schedule to keep, Closon might have probed further into such a mistake, but today, time and the wind were equally precious. "As you are new with our crew, I shall overlook the fault of your tardiness, just this once. See that it does not happen again. You will find me strict, but just. Perform your duties as I expect and you shall be well rewarded. Fail me, and you shall never set foot again on my ship, nor any other belonging to my master, the Marquis de Blaise."

The captain watched the new man's eyes to gauge his reaction. Closon always found it useful to mention the name of the man whom he ultimately served, in order to overawe those new to his service. He found it encouraged the ambitious and cowed the shirkers.

Lacombe stood ramrod straight. "I understand, Capitaine."

Closon read through Lacombe's papers again as he considered how best to put the new man to use. "Your service record indicates you've served aboard merchantmen before. What other vessels have you sailed on?"

"The *Oliphant*, out of Brest. She was my latest employment. Before that I worked on slavers mostly. In charge of ship security and keeping the vermin in check." Lacombe seemed nervous in his answer, as if he had trouble in remembering.

Closon raised an eyebrow. "Vermin?"

Lacombe broke into a half grin, displaying an upper row of perfect, even teeth. "The *Nègres*, sir."

Closon sat back in his chair. Something about the man standing before him didn't seem to fit. Lacombe had a compact medium build, with a tough-looking slant to his handsome face, which seemed to caution anyone against taking him lightly. His service record, at least the part of it recorded in his papers, indicated a long and distinguished record of performance, but Closon knew by long experience that written records often didn't tell the whole story about a man. They omitted things like judgement, character and leadership. Important qualities in managing men aboard a ship. Qualities which tended to surface or disappear in a crisis. What would this Lacombe be like under real duress? Could he be trusted in the middle of the Atlantic in a gale? Or to keep a hungry, tired and overworked crew in line? Closon struggled to put his finger on the missing piece Lacombe's puzzle.

A loud knocking interrupted his thoughts. Closon turned his head toward the door, anticipating the face of his second in command. "Enter. Ah, it's you, Reveillon."

"Forgive the intrusion, Capitaine. You asked me to notify you as soon as all the cargo had been secured and we had wind enough to get underway. Shall I give the order to prepare for departure?"

Closon looked from Reveillon to Lacombe and then promptly decided on both matters put before him. "Yes, Lieutenant, and take Lacombe here with you. He's to join our crew as Quartermaster and Officer of the Watch. Monsieur Lacombe, meet my number two, Lieutenant Pierre Reveillon."

Lacombe stuck out his hand. "An honor to meet you, Lieutenant."

Reveillon shook hands and gave Lacombe a nod of welcome. "Welcome aboard."

As Closon folded up Lacombe's papers, he noticed a faded smudge at the corner of the neatly written document, which looked like blood. He rubbed at it with a finger, then shook his head with disdain, pointing out the stain to Lacombe. "Lieutenant, I want all officers and crew ready for inspection in one hour. Mister Lacombe, if I don't find your personal effects in better order than these papers, you'll be swabbing the decks with the rest of the common crew. I won't have such careless blemishes about my ship. Understood?"

"Aye, Capitaine!" Lacombe said smartly.

Closon handed back the smudged papers. Lacombe saluted and folded them with care, tucking them inside the inner pocket of his jacket. Closon stood with his hands behind his back. The interview had ended. "Lieutenant Reveillon will show you the ropes. Now out of my sight the both of you. I have real work to do."

*

Lacombe nodded followed the lieutenant out of the cabin and onto the main deck. The sun shone brightly overhead. *How did I miss that little blotch?* Never mind, he had passed the first test in his assumed role. *Putain! But the old bugger had me worried. For a second there I feared he saw through me, but in the end, my luck held. What's more, I'll be in charge of dispersing pay and policing the ship as well! It's the perfect job for a man of my talents.*

Lacombe put his arms behind his back to mimic the images he'd seen in paintings of naval officers. He dutifully followed Reveillon about as the lieutenant introduced him to the other members of the crew. Wherever Reveillon led him, Lacombe smiled, flattered, and oozed all the charm he could muster to win the confidence of his new shipmates. He knew how to fawn and play any fool false. He'd had a lifetime of practice at deception. His looks always helped. People liked it when you were handsome. They wanted to put their faith in you and often did, right up until the point when you stabbed them in the back or sliced open their gut. Ah, to see the shock in their eyes as the knife went in and with the last stuttering breaths of life, the victim realized his betrayal. What a marvelous thing to behold. Of course, by then it was too late for most of them to even scream.

Lacombe grinned at the advantages of his current situation. If he reaped half as much profit on this venture as the real Lacombe had promised, he might even be able to rejoin his old gang in Bigorre. If he returned with enough gold, even those old cutthroats would let bygones be bygones, despite the fact he'd stolen from them. He hadn't wanted to do it, but he'd needed money to avoid a trip back to prison and the puke in charge of guarding the gang's stash had resisted handing it over. He had slit the poor fool's throat for his recalcitrance, a necessary but regrettable act which had forced him to go on the run from both his old comrades and the police. While running, he'd lived the high life until most of what he'd taken had been pissed away on whores, gambling, and wine. The little he had left bought him passage to Marseilles.

Ah, the good old days, Malveau reminisced. He cradled the sharp dirk hidden in the pocket of his waistcoat—his one true friend. *One step at a time*, he cautioned himself. The bright sunlight felt good against his face as he began to circle the deck on his first patrol. *Slay the shepherd first, and then all the lambs will be there for the taking.* He began to whistle an easy tune as he started on his rounds, and made a silent vow, to make himself a prince among his fellow murderers and thieves, no matter the price in villainy and blood.

*

Johan Peter Vesterkamp had only one expression, or so it seemed to Nicolas; a long uninterrupted scowl, often followed by a grunt of disdain. Nicolas got the look now, as Vesterkamp nodded toward a set of fencing equipment laid out on a table at the end of the salon. "Play time is over now, boy. You've been here long enough. Show me what you've learned, and I warn you, if you displease me, I'll stick you like a suckling pig."

Vesterkamp pointed at a cavalry saber, a broad, heavy weapon, difficult to use and not routinely given to apprentices for training purposes. Nicolas picked it up, turning the leather-wrapped iron hilt in his hand. The edge looked sharp enough to cut through flesh and bone. Nicolas put on the doublet and gaunts set out for him. He had no protective mask. He swung the saber for balance and feel with his right hand and took up a neutral fighting stance.

Vesterkamp already wore armor. He had a saber in his right hand as well. Nicolas wondered if the edge had been honed to the same sharpness as his own blade. If so, he would need to be very careful. Vesterkamp gave the ritual salute between combatants before an engagement. He narrowed his eyes as he watched Nicolas. Nicolas knew the fight had already begun.

"Right, boy. Attack me!"

Nicolas launched himself at the fencing master. He slashed and cut ferociously, but his blade tasted only sweat-laden air. Vesterkamp parried the incoming attacks with seeming ease, brushing each cut and thrust aside. Nicolas lost his balance in a lunge. Vesterkamp threw him over onto his back. Nicolas rolled away and got to his feet, turning to adopt a side stance, left foot forward, the hand guard of the blade even with his mouth, point angled up and behind him. Vesterkamp raised his right arm and pointed his sword at Nicolas' left eye. Nicolas extended his sword arm and aimed the tip of his blade at his master's throat to counter. He leaned forward form the shoulder, inviting an attack.

The sword master spread both arms wide to the side, making a human cross. "Good. You didn't take the bait. Now show me what you can do."

Nicolas began again, but with more measured attacks in connected series. He probed at the flanks, attacking Vesterkamp's legs, looking for a weak point in timing or stance, but found none. As each attack ended, he had to be ready for Vesterkamp's own counter, defeat it, clear into neutral space, and begin again. The two swordsmen settled into a rhythm; the flat ping as steel came together, mixed with the stamp and shuffle of feet and the occasional grunts of effort as each man lunged, parried, and cut at each other. The ominous whistle of each blade slicing through air gave way to sparks when the edges made contact. Nicolas had never felt so hard pressed.

The salon used a converted barn with a stone floor for its practice space. The interior still reeked of animal sweat and leavings, but the large space gave the fencers the room they needed to practice. The beams had been rigged to hold chandeliers which could be hauled up to provide light in the evening, though the men rarely came to train in the evening, preferring other pleasures of the night. The walls were lined with hooks and shelves of equipment covered the back and side walls. The hay loft had been converted into a place for the men to sleep in barracks style, and the high windows in the loft provided ample light during the day for training when the big front doors stood open. Other practice encounters had been underway in the long rectangular space, but as the length and ferocity of the contest between the salon master and his new pupil grew, the other swordsmen gradually halted their own bouts to get a better view of the intriguing contest.

Vesterkamp parried a cut and then lunged at Nicolas. Nicolas barely managed to turn his body and the blade aside, to avoid being run through. Vesterkamp looked surprised that his attack had not landed a touch.

One of the salon veterans observing the bout turned to the man standing next to him. "Have you ever seen Vesterkamp tested so? By a mere boy from the looks of him."

The question came from Philippe Noitier de Mauran, third son of the Comte de Mauran and holder of the honorary title of Vidame de Saint-Dié. Mauran had never set foot in the diocese of which he held the office of protector and little in his character deemed him suitable for such duties, should he ever have wished to perform them. Vain, short of stature and temper, but handsome, urbane, bored, debauched—his favorite pastimes included drinking, hunting, and whoring, in no particular order and preferably all three together. When not engaged in ruining himself in the pursuit of these vices, he could usually be found attempting to seduce the daughters of the local gentry with false promises of enduring love and grand estates. He enjoyed enough success with his deceptions to have need of some skill with a sword to defend himself in the duels which inevitably followed, once the fathers and brothers of the girls he ruined discovered the truth of his conduct. Mauran sired at least four brats, which he knew of. Their disgraced mothers left all of them on the steps of local orphanages. He felt nothing for the spoiled mothers or his unwanted children. He expected to add two more brats to the collection, if the milkmaid at the inn and his aunt's new housekeeper were to be believed. The milkmaid had no siblings to defend her, and had an aged and helpless father, but the housekeeper had a brother who served several years in the cavalry and had a reputation as being well-versed with a blade. Mauran needed to practice in case the man came after him. He came regularly to the *Salon du Fer to* train, because they only admitted the best bladesmen.

The man to whom Mauran had posed the question, followed the ebb and flow of the bout with keen interest. "I've never seen anyone push him so hard. Who on earth do you suppose that boy is, and where did he acquire such skill?"

"He's the Chevalier d'Argentolle, the youngest son of the Marquis de Blaise. He arrived only a few days ago in the company of his elder brother, the Comte de Marbéville."

Mauran looked over at the tall, thin man standing to his left who had answered the question. He had the nervous scampering manner of a ferret, his eyes and head movements quick and constantly darting about.

"Guy de Montbatre," the man said, providing his own introduction as he inserted himself into the conversation. "I remember him because I'm new to the salon as well. I arrived just after he did and heard him mentioning his particulars."

Mauran snorted his disdain as his eye continued to follow the match. "Another dilettante young nobleman out for fun and adventure, eh? Well, he'd best be careful. Vesterkamp's a mean old sod and not one to be trifled with. If the boy shows too much youthful arrogance, he may wind up with more than he bargained for."

Mauran's warning appeared prescient as Nicolas rushed in with a lunge to try to exploit an opening in Vesterkamp's guard. The Dutch master slid his saber along the line of attack, and then pivoted, smacking Nicolas hard on the side of the head with the hilt the blade.

The force of the blow, struck Nicolas flush on the ear. He reeled backwards, got his feet tangled and crashed hard into the column of an old stone chimney behind him. Mauran led the chorus of low derision aimed at the newcomer. Many at the salon seemed relieved to see the new man finally humbled.

Undaunted by the amusement he appeared to be providing for some, Nicolas fought to regain his equilibrium. He shook the ringing from his head and pressed back into the fray. His arms and legs ached from the effort, but he ignored the fatigue and the pain from the many welts and bruises Vesterkamp gave him each time he countered. Nicolas knew he couldn't match the master. Had it been a real bout, he would already have been run through—several times, but Vesterkamp wished to test him, not kill him. Vesterkamp wasn't trying to show how good he was. He wanted to find out about Nicolas, and not just if he possessed any talent with the blade. Resilience, character, determination, the ability to think and adapt on one's feet, to find a way to solve one's own problems; these traits were usually far more important than skill alone, and could only be truly measured in the crucible of combat.

Nicolas' lungs burned from the effort of keeping Vesterkamp at bay. He couldn't last much longer. Time to show the salon master what he was made of, one way, or the other, before he exhausted himself. Nicolas gulped in air through his mouth and took several steps backward to give himself a breathing space. He let his shoulders slump so that Vesterkamp would think him exhausted. Just as the Dutchman stepped forward to begin another attack, Nicolas surged in with a rapid vicious counterattack, his blade alternately thrusting and cutting with increasing swiftness in a technique all of his own he dubbed the 'butterfly's sting.' The unexpected ferocity of the advance disconcerted Vesterkamp enough for Nicolas to force a small opening. He landed a blow, which sliced through the padded doublet of Vesterkamp's left shoulder, drawing blood.

The onlookers gasped. Most had never laid a successful touch upon the master in a bout. The boy they watched had drawn blood. The watchers remained glued to the scene of combat, anticipating the inevitable reaction from the salon master. They did not have long to wait.

Vesterkamp rushed forward. He surged through Nicolas' attempted defenses and rewarded his pupil with a blow from the brass hand guard of his saber, straight to the face. The force of the blow lifted Nicolas off his feet and left him sprawled and dazed on the floor of the salon.

Mauran let out a loud guffaw. Vesterkamp turned and glared at him, then inspected the tear-shaped blood spot on his left shoulder with visible disgust. He walked over to the corner to retrieve the bucket of well water used to revive those knocked senseless during training. The other members of the salon pressed in close to fill the space left by the two combatants.

*

Vesterkamp heard the shuffling of feet behind him, and then voices hushed in surprise. He turned, bucket in hand, to see Nicolas staggering to his feet.

"I thank you for the offer of refreshment, Monsieur, but it will not be necessary. Too much water and I'm afraid I'll have to go piss."

The hard men among the veterans of the salon nodded to each other in silence, impressed at the bravado of the young swordsman. Others looked on warily, unsure as to how the salon master would respond. If he judged the boy's words too proud, would a real bout now be in the offing? No one laughed now.

Vesterkamp took a cold unflinching look at Nicolas. He bled from the nose and lip, and Vesterkamp suspected the inside of the boy's mouth oozed blood. *I'm sure he's never received a blow like the one I gave him. Where's his gentleman's outrage? I've done my best to goad him on. He must have a dozen welts on his skin beneath those fine clothes. He should be enraged, cursing and threatening like the rest of these fools, yet he stands there with calm defiance, ready to engage again. Can't he tell when he's beaten? Or perhaps, unlike the rest of this sorry lot, he knows enough not to care.*

The salon master and his pupil locked eyes. Each attempted to stare the other down. The sparring had been just a physical exercise. With the boy's lack of experience compared to his own, of course it could only end one way. Now the real struggle began. *I sense neither anger nor fear. Just a calm alertness and readiness—what my own master called the 'no-mind.' How astounding to find an adept in such a place!*

Vesterkamp had served for many years on the island of Dejima in Japan, where he had learned from noted Christian samurai, the techniques and philosophies of Japanese swordsmanship. These techniques formed the basis of his success as a fencing master. After years of failing to find a suitable apprentice to whom he could pass on his methods and secrets, thought he would take them with him to the grave. Now he began to wonder.

The master swordsman looked through Nicolas. He knew the rumors of his questionable heritage. To Vesterkamp, only white men really counted for something. All the other races deserved only contempt. Yet, he admired the boy before him because he showed courage and talent. For just the second time in his life, Vesterkamp questioned the validity of his long held beliefs. *You laughed at the*

Japaners too when you first landed on Dejima, called them little monkeys, didn't you? Well look what those 'monkeys' taught you. What would you be now without them? Is this boy made of the same mettle as they?

Blood streamed down Nicolas' nose, mouth, and chin onto the floor, leaving bright red stains. *Can't swallow fast enough to stop it oozing from your mouth now, can you*? Vesterkamp knew what that felt like. He'd been there too. Samurai teaching methods showed no reluctance to shed blood. *Pain is rice. Blood is sake. If you want to live by the sword, you need to consume lots of both.* His own master used to say. Most would have walked out by now, made their excuses and fled, but still the boy stood there, stubborn and proud, and ready to fight, just as he himself had done.

Vesterkamp made his decision. He lowered his blade. "I think we've done enough for today."

The master glanced dismissively toward Mauran, raking his eyes across the faces of the others who had also dared to mock his young opponent. "You've done well, boy. Not many of this lot have ever laid a touch on me."

Vesterkamp fetched a towel, which he soaked in the cold water, then walked over to Nicolas. The chevalier lowered his sword arm with caution. Vesterkamp held the back of Nicolas' head with his left hand and with his right, took the damp towel and began almost tenderly, to wipe the blood from Nicolas' face. "Hold it there like this, lad. It'll help stop the bleeding. The cold stings, but it helps with the pain. Today you've passed the first test. Tomorrow your real lessons begin."

*

The *Salon de Fer* sat just outside the town of Ducos on Martinique. Despite its humble appearance, the salon ranked as the most celebrated académie of swordsmanship in the West Indies. The routine of training each day remained constant and demanding, and Vesterkamp, the salon master, made it even more so for Nicolas.

The chevalier arrived before the sun rose, performing his drill and combat stances under the watchful guidance of his master. At the end of morning drill, Nicolas completed a precise series of a thousand prescribed cuts with each arm— a requirement which left his muscles so sore over the first weeks of training he could barely lift his arms above his shoulders. Once he had completed his individual drill, Nicolas joined the general morning session, where he would observe the various fencers as they faced off against each other, studying the movements and habits of each man— seeing much, understanding little, but determined to prepare himself for the day when he might stand in their respective places. After a brief midday pause to eat and rest, Nicolas began his afternoon session, where he practiced footwork for hours without touching any of the weapons. The rest of the participants dismissed at four o'clock, at which time Nicolas began again another round of personal instruction using daggers and close-in weapons. He also practiced fighting from the saddle, which began at six and lasted until eight o'clock each night. Only when darkness made it too dangerous to continue his training did Vesterkamp allow the young chevalier to return to his lodgings.

The onset of night, however, provided Nicolas with no respite from his labors. After a brief break for a Spartan supper at the nearby inn where he lodged, Monsignor Arnaud arrived with books under arm to tutor him in preparation for his entry into the École Militaire. If Nicolas worked diligently, he could conclude his studies by midnight, at which time he would step into the bath his valet had prepared for him to enjoy the only unguarded period of relaxation throughout the entire day. Afterward, before he went to bed, Nicolas would read any mail from Sérolène which had arrived, and write his own letter of response.

No matter how spent or sore he felt, Sérolène's letters always lifted his spirits, providing the unquestioned highlight of the day. Despite their separation, the frequent exchange of unfiltered communications allowed them both to gradually discover the endlessly mundane assortment of intimate minutiae, which no one except a lover desires to know about anyone else. Favorite colors, books, sweets, pastimes—secret dislikes, fears, and nicknames—amusing things they could do with fingers, toes, and ears—children's names they preferred—heroes they admired and composers they adored. On the many threads of these small, shared confidences, their shared love grew ever deeper, despite the physical distance which separated them.

Before he extinguished the day's last candle, Nicolas always wrote his promised daily missive to his beloved, describing his day and anything of interest which might come to mind. The letters always ended with Nicolas telling Sérolène over and over how much he adored and missed her. Sleep came quickly, as soon as he affixed seal to paper. On more than one occasion Julius, Nicolas' valet, found his master asleep at his desk, quill in hand, too exhausted to make it the final few feet to his bed.

For more than three months, Nicolas endured the grueling rigors of unfaltering routine. The requirements of Vesterkamp's style proved so physically demanding that Nicolas often ended the day not just exhausted, but also covered in slashes and cuts from the exacting training. Nicolas excelled not only with the blade, but on the firing range at practice with musket and rifle as well. He loved riding the most, however, learning the intricacies of guiding his mounts with just the barest prompting of his legs and feet, how to shoot from the saddle with musket and pistol, and the nuances of the Austrian dressage. Nicolas had no days off, not even on Sundays, which were given over wholly to Monsignor Arnaud.

The effort produced rewards. Along with a superbly honed body, Nicolas notched a steady stream of victories over all opponents. By the end of the second month, his skill had grown to such an extent that few swordsmen provided a challenge in single combat. Vesterkamp solved the problem of adequate competition by pitting Nicolas against multiple adversaries, starting with two and then increasing the number until he found the desired point of 'battle equilibrium,' somewhere between seven and ten simultaneous opponents.

Many of the men, having lost several times to Nicolas and with no more excuses to make, engaged with him only when compelled to. Most took their defeats in stride, aware of Nicolas' growing reputation. But a few seemed unable to accept the chevalier's ascent, resenting Nicolas' skill and the special instruction he received.

A cabal of resentful plotters soon developed in the salon, led by Mauran and Montbatre. The latter proved himself very adept at stirring the resentment of the other men by inventing slights and boasts which he attributed falsely to Nicolas. By painting the chevalier as the villain, Montbatre cemented his influence stone by spiteful stone. At night, when Nicolas spent company with Monsignor Arnaud and his books, the ne'er-do-wells passed the time indulging in whatever illicit pleasures could be found near Ducos. The nightly dissipations became fertile ground to further stoke resentment against Nicolas. Montbatre plied his salon comrades with wine and poisoned their ears and hearts against the chevalier with skillfully manufactured calumnies.

Had Montbatre's group of pretenders possessed any shred of integrity, challenges would have been issued and matters settled honorably, with apologies or blades. They preferred, however, to sulk rather than fight. Shamming themselves wronged, they seethed from the sidelines. Provocateurs and posers, the lurked about full of angry looks and bold glances, but never dared more whenever Nicolas approached.

Tired of the poisonous atmosphere, Vesterkamp determined to settle matters once, and for all. He staged a bout between Nicolas and Mauran, the best fencer among the malcontents and their nominal leader. The entire salon assembled to witness the bout. Vesterkamp himself would oversee it. Montbatre brought the news to his cabal on Monday evening, as the ne'er do wells spent the night in Ducos' best whorehouse. Mauran seemed eager for the contest, vowing to teach the chevalier a lesson on the morrow, when the bout would be held. Montbatre wrote a letter to Ginestas the same night, informing the baron that their plans seemed to be well ahead of schedule and he hoped the baron would remember him their employers.

*

The next morning, the entire membership of the salon, some forty men in all, gathered in assembly to witness the contest. Vesterkamp stood before a waist high table. On it lay a freshly sharpened cavalry saber, the blade withdrawn from the scabbard and gleaming with a fresh coat of oil. "The contest will be fought with sabers. Monsieur de Mauran, here is your weapon. Go to the wall and select your protective gear."

141

Mauran took up the saber, admiring the fine blade. He sheathed it then went to put on his gear. As his made his way through a gauntlet of onlookers, the sword master leaned his head toward a rack of wooden blades against the far wall. "Nicolas, you may take your weapon from among those over there. You shall fight with nothing more than your shirt for protection. In order to win, you must score sixteen touches. Mauran, need score only one."

A low murmur rumbled from the throats of the men of the salon, newcomers and veterans alike. The unbalanced nature of the weapons seemed only to add to the feeling of unequal treatment. The men of Montbatre's circle looked to him for a response.

Montbatre stepped forward to protest. "Surely such conditions are excessive. Your regulations make a mockery of the contest, Monsieur, given the unevenness of the terms and the weapons. I beg you to reconsider, and administer the bout with rules equal to the skill and dignity of both gentlemen."

Vesterkamp stared at Montbatre. None of the longstanding regulars would ever have dared to challenge his teachings or his rules. The salon belonged to him and he could do as he pleased. All who entered did so by his leave. That Montbatre would dare to speak out in so public a fashion spoke a good deal toward the damage he and his compatriots had already done to the moral fabric of the salon. Vesterkamp let the great space of the salon fill with silence, before he gave his reply.

"As you point out, Monsieur, it is a contest and not a duel. I can therefore set the terms as I see fit. But perhaps you are right. I should even things out a bit, shouldn't I, so each man receives his proper due," Vesterkamp said in a conciliatory manner.

Montbatre bowed to acknowledge the master's concession. A grin of satisfaction teased about the edges of his mouth. Vesterkamp could read his thoughts. Montbatre knew his influence would grow in the salon. A reward for being bold enough to have dared confront the salon master directly.

Vesterkamp swept his gaze across the cabal of dissidents standing behind Montbatre. "Nicolas, sixteen's too easy. Make it an even twenty."

Montbatre stepped back as if he'd been slapped, a look of shock mixed with humiliation cascaded rapidly across his face. The rest of the watching swordsmen exchanged curious glances, but no one ventured any further comments. It seemed most weren't sure whether Vesterkamp intended good or ill for Nicolas.

Mauran returned to the center of the gathering, ready to begin the combat. He faced up to Vesterkamp, his gaze speaking to all the men gathered. "You mock me, Monsieur, you, and your special favorite. Since you are so confident, I will accept your terms. Today I will show you what *I* am capable of. Your pet will learn a lesson in humility and you will learn the degree to which you have greatly neglected my talent."

Vesterkamp snorted at the boast. "Don't tell me. Show me,"

*

Nicolas stood to Vesterkamp's right as the master moved to the center point of the lane in which the bout would be contested. Nicolas had listened to everything said, but remained silent. Only the overture had been played. The curtain had yet to be raised on the main act. His master had

143

dictated the piece to be played and thinking about the odds
or the number of touches he needed to score wouldn't help
him. He had to concentrate and manage the fight. One
mistake could mean his defeat and Mauran's saber had a
very sharp edge. A touch might even prove fatal if he wasn't
vigilant and he knew Mauran would be wholly unconcerned
with doing him injury. Though the bout wasn't technically a
duel, it had all the requisite trappings of one, bad blood and
all.

Nicolas walked back to his starting position and
concentrated on his breathing. He entered a state of
conscious emptiness, preparing his body to fight. Lifting his
wooden sword in salute, he took an open stance at the far end
of the salon, feet beneath his shoulders and evenly balanced.
His sword lay pointed down in his right hand, within the line
of his body.

Mauran turned to his left side and extended his left arm
forward, the sword in his right hand slight withdrawn and
below the line of his left arm. Vesterkamp stood in the
middle of the combatants. He looked from one man to the
next, his right hand raised high overhead.

"En garde." Vesterkamp dropped his arm and stepped
back out of the line of engagement. "Begin!"

*

Nicolas ran forward, smacked Mauran's blade up and
to his right and landed a thrust on the left shoulder just above
the heart. "First touch to the chevalier! Halt. Return to your
positions."

Both combatants moved to comply, but Mauran
seemed greatly unsettled by the ferocity of Nicolas' attack,
and the seeming ease with which the first touch had been

144

landed. Nicolas took up the exact same stance as before, his eyes obscure green pools. He moved the tip of his sword across his body. The point still aimed at the ground. Mauran eyes seemed glued to his blade.

"Begin!"

Nicolas surged forward again, the point low until the last moment. Mauran lunged forward in a heavy thrust, his weight too far forward. Nicolas brought his fist toward his own face, rode the thrust and then extended his arm, catching Mauran flush on the throat. Mauran gagged and fell to his knees.

Vesterkamp stepped between the combatants. "Second touch to the chevalier. Halt. Resume positions."

The bout resumed. In under three minutes, Nicolas landed ten more touches, despite the disadvantages of a wooden blade and no protection against a live one. Mauran sweated profusely, lashing out as his rage and embarrassment took over, desperate to land any touch at all to preserve his honor as the points against him piled up and his exhaustion and frustration mounted. Nicolas, in contrast, seemed to flow with ease into each thrust and parry. Whereas Mauran huffed and puffed, bending over in exhaustion and the bout wore on, Nicolas hardly seemed to breathe.

At sixteen touches, Mauran asked for the favor of a brief respite so he could relieve himself, giving the excuse of having drunk too much wine with his midday meal as reason for his poor showing. When, after ten minutes, he had still failed to return from the privy, Vesterkamp sent one of the men to fetch him back. In less than a minute, the man came trooping back, a mocking grin upon his face.

"Our bird has flown the coop. His horse is gone too," the man reported.

Vesterkamp turned to address the other men assembled. "Nicolas is declared the winner by default. Mauran's cowardice has brought shame to himself and his compatriots. He is no longer welcome here, and neither are they."

The salon master stared pointedly at Montbatre and the others standing near him. "All of you get out."

The men encompassed by Vesterkamp's gaze turned with disdain and made their way out of the salon.

As soon as they had gone, Vesterkamp made a show of taking in several big breaths of air. "Phew. Now it doesn't stink anymore, with those vermin gone."

He raked his eyes across the faces of those remaining. "If there are any others who wish to join Mauran and his band, you can leave now too."

No one moved. "Any doubts left about the ability of the chevalier? If so, I invite you to step forward and take Mauran's place. Same generous terms as before."

No one came forward or made any sound. "Back to your drills, then. We've wasted enough time today."

The men went back to their work. Vesterkamp turned toward Nicolas, who waited with wooden sword in hand, for instructions. "Damned sloppy of you, Nicolas. I expected better. I want a thousand cuts with each arm, diagonals across the chest. You can do each arm at the same time and practice your two-sword technique. I can see there's no more point in trying this lot in single combat anymore. Off with you, boy."

Nicolas turned away without a word and moved off toward the corner to begin his drills. He didn't sulk with being given more work to do. He had learned that his master preferred to give work as a substitute for spoken praise. The more pleased he was, the more work he assigned.

Vesterkamp watched Nicolas go, satisfied with what he had seen in the bout and delighted by what he hadn't seen in the aftermath. Nicolas hadn't gloated in victory, nor had he expected praise or pouted at not finding it. *Your reward out there is staying alive, boy. That's all the accolade you'll ever need.*

*

On the last day of May, Nicolas came to the salon to train as usual but found it deserted. He went around the back to check for anything amiss and saw a note posted on the rear door, directing him to an address further up the narrow road from the salon. Nicolas mounted up and rode to the location indicated, which turned out to be a shabby one-story house. All but one of the front windows had been broken and then patched with wood, the shutters dangling unevenly from the broken sills.

Tying his mount to a post, Nicolas knocked on the door, waiting with patience for someone to answer. The neighborhood the house stood in could best be described as happily seedy. Had he ridden in on the docile mare Aemilia, he might have been concerned about leaving his horse unattended, but he chuckled to himself at the thought of a stranger getting anywhere near Scipio, let alone attempting to mount him. The large black steed earned a reputation at every stable Nicolas housed him in for his bad temper and surliness at being handled by anyone save his master and accustomed grooms.

Nicolas heard a muffled shout from inside the building, followed by the breaking of glass. A man swore loudly. A high-pitched voice shouted back.

"To hell with you too, you shit!"

The door flew open and a woman, half-undressed and struggling to put on the remainder of her clothes, appeared in the doorway, almost colliding with him in her rush to leave. Nicolas removed his hat and bowed as a courtesy, though it seemed obvious she must be a professional plying her trade. She leaned over so both breasts tumbled out over the top of her loose bodice, eying him coyly as she displayed her wares without embarrassment. A stray lock of dark brown hair fell loosely across her left eye. She brushed it back in place, grinning all the while, her gaze sharp and calculating, with the look of someone long used to sizing up the worth of her potential companions in an instant.

"Hello there, sweetie. My my, but aren't you the handsome one."

Nicolas couldn't be sure if the throaty whisper of her voice had been manufactured in an effort to sound alluring, not that it mattered. Her breath smelled of cheap rum and rotting teeth. Nicolas turned his head aside to avoid the stench.

The fallen flower seemed to understand a no sale sign when she saw it. She huffed, pulling on a loose blue petticoat to cover herself up. "Suit yourself, then!"

Nicolas watched her storm off into the early dawn streets, the clatter of her wooden sabots gradually diminishing till the faded scent of cheap perfume and woman sweat remained the only remnant of her passing. Vesterkamp filled the narrow doorway with his bulk, an open bottle of

148

rum in his sword hand. Nicolas immediately forgot about the woman.

Vesterkamp took a long swig from the bottle, then tossed the drained container to the ground. "You're early, as usual. Come on in. I have something for you."

Nicolas entered the untidy interior of the small house, amazed at the mess and the squalor. There lay everywhere—some unopened, some smashed, others tipped over and lying haphazardly about the room. The remnants of a meal lay on a worn and chipped table in the corner of the main room, swarmed by a cloud of flies. The room itself had only a small bed with some very dirty-looking linen, a worn old sofa, and a single wooden chair.

Vesterkamp brushed aside the debris on the floor with his foot, making a path for them to walk through as he led Nicolas into the back room. In contrast to the squalid and unkempt nature of the first room, this second room, though smaller, had been kept spotless and tidy. One of its walls held edged weapons of all types, with a neat row of specially constructed shelves built to house the armaments, some of which appeared expensive and, Nicolas assumed, quite rare. The opposite wall held firearms, kept in the same precise order and pristine condition as the blades.

At the end of the room stood a large set of armor, but of a type Nicolas had never before seen. The shape looked like an extended triangle and the armored plates had been painted red with green trimming. The helmet sloped toward the shoulders like a pyramid, with an iron mask at the center decorated by a long bristled moustache made of straw.

Nicolas turned toward his master. "That armor is superb! May I ask where you came by it, Monsieur?"

"It's from Japan. I acquired it during my years in the Dutch Marines."

Vesterkamp invited Nicolas to sit on one of the two stools, the only other furniture in the room. As he took his seat, Nicolas noticed a neat and precisely folded bedroll in the corner, of the type cavalrymen carried on their saddles. He waited with patience for his master to continue. Vesterkamp had never before volunteered an ounce of information about himself, and Nicolas still had no idea why he had been summoned, or what the old soldier intended by his summons.

Vesterkamp glanced about the room. To Nicolas he seemed suddenly aware of the general squalor. He bunched his fists together and then let his hands relax, staring down at the backs of gnarled and scarred fingers. "I never did feel ashamed of how I live now. But seeing you here, makes it feel different. It might sound absurd to you, Nicolas, but somehow you remind me of the promise I once had, before drink, hard luck, and poor choices consumed it all.

Vesterkamp peered out the open doorway toward the squalid main room of the house. "I told that tramp she wasn't to come in here. She has no place else to go, so I let her stay here from time to time, when she can't find a cock to pay for it. Trouble is, she's too stupid to listen when she gets drunk. That's her room out there and you see the mess she makes of it. Mine's in here. She's off to ply her trade now. Scrounge out a living as best she can. God's blood, I don't know why I keep with her. I suppose even a stone needs some company from time to time, eh?"

Nicolas didn't know what to say, so he remained respectfully silent. Vesterkamp seemed grateful he didn't say anything stupid or condescending in reply. Nicolas had learned over months of training, that silence had meaning too. Swordsmen often spoke to each other on its waves. Vesterkamp stared down at his hands, then looked up at Nicolas. "That's one of your talents, boy. You know when not to disturb the silence."

Vesterkamp watched Nicolas watching him. "You also no how to listen. Another important trait. People come here wanting easy answers. How do I kill man without getting killed, or maimed? Well there's no easy answer to that one. And even if there were, half these fools wouldn't hear it if you shouted right in their ears. But you, you were still just clay and raw material when you arrived here. A sword starts the same way. Now, you've been hammered and tempered into something much harder and more durable. Your training has forged you, folded you over and over again, then and heated and beaten out the impurities, so when given a proper polish, your edge will cut like nothing else. Just like these blades."

The swordsman turned on his stool to admire the collection behind him. Some swords wore full dress scabbards, the polished sheen of the lacquer shining in the light of early morning. Others slept in unadorned wooden sheaths.

"Not bad, the blades those yellow monkeys could make. I think they're the finest he world has ever seen," Vesterkamp said.

"Such craftsmanship. I don't believe I've ever seen anything quite like them. Are they all from Japan?" Nicolas asked.

Vesterkamp turned to face Nicolas again. "Yes, and this brings us to the point of why you're here."

The sword master went to the rack and took down a one of the swords, drawing out the blade several inches to reveal the stunning quality of the tempered steel. The hardened edge glinted as the morning light reflected off it through a hole in the patched bedroom window.

Vesterkamp withdrew the blade fully from its scabbard. "In Japan, they say a sword has a soul of its own. They know a thing or two about steel, those bastards. I've seen swords of theirs cut through armor, flesh, and bone, and come out the other side without a nick. Nothing else compares to the best of their blades. Not even Toledo steel."

Nicolas couldn't tear his gaze away from the blade which had a wave-like pattern tempering line in the steel, running the full length of the sword. Vesterkamp returned the sword to its sheath and placed it back upon the rack. "Superb, isn't it? It's ironic that a thing used to kill could be so beautiful."

Vesterkamp returned to his stool and fixed Nicolas with his gaze. "The warriors in Japan make a god of death. They fear nothing but dishonor. The sword, which represents their soul, is everything to them. You have many similar qualities, boy. They also believe a sword chooses its owner, not the other way around."

Vesterkamp turned his head and nodded toward the wall behind him. "You are the finest student I've ever trained. I've driven you hard these past few months because I wanted to teach you the secrets I learned in Japan, and I knew we hadn't much time. I've taught you all I know. The only thing missing is a good sword, one that will help you live long enough to gain the experience you will need to put what you have learned to proper use. The right sword will help you to master the forms you've been taught and yourself in the process."

Vesterkamp stood and folded his arms against his chest. "Your last lesson, Nicolas, is to let one of those swords choose you."

*

Nicolas stared at his master. He had never expected the type of test he encountered now. He stood at his master's prompting and surveyed the various swords on the rack. Some of them seemed so splendid in their colorful scabbards. Like jewels of war. *But which one is for me?*

"Let your intuition be your guide, Nicolas. Only then will your choice be a wise one," Vesterkamp said.

Nicolas reached for a blade in a brilliantly decorated red scabbard, his eyes drawn to the lustrous colors of the lacquer. His hand almost touched the scabbard, when he stopped himself, eyes drawn to a pile of swords in the corner, standing on end. The handles protruded out from under a rough cotton cloth used to cover them. Many looked to be used for spare parts, as some of the fittings on the sword guards and handles were missing. As he moved closer to get a better look, Nicolas noticed a sword in a plain, slightly battered wooden scabbard. This sword stood longer than the rest, and had a more pronounced curvature. Nicolas felt himself oddly drawn to it. He glanced at Vesterkamp to see if the corner swords were forbidden to him, but the swordsman said nothing, just continued to watch him intently.

Nicolas took silence for encouragement. He reached for the blade and lifted it out of the pile. It felt somehow right in his hand. The weight, length, feel and balance seemed ideal, and he knew he had found *his* blade, that he had made the right choice. The only choice.

Nicolas held the sword toward his master. "This one."

Vesterkamp began to chuckle, a deep low rumble. Nicolas sensed an edge to it. Vesterkamp shook his head, exhaling with a long sigh. "God's blood, I might have known. The Muramasa."

"The what?" Nicolas asked.

"Muramasa is the name of its maker. Legend has it the swordsmith was both a genius and a madman. They say he imparted part of his spirit to each of the blades he made. You've chosen well. The Japaners say there is nothing on earth that cuts like the demon swords of Muramasa. Be warned, they are also rumored to be thirsty for blood. Beware the power of their call."

Nicolas unsheathed the sword slowly, awed by the flawless quality of the steel, so dark it seemed almost deep blue. The pattern of tempering atop the razor-sharp edge of the blade looked like alternating mountain plateaus. The blade had a carving on the steel toward the hilt. On one side an exquisite etching of a tiger had been engraved. On the other, talons clutched a spear. Nicolas felt a chill go through him, recalling the tale his brother told of an eagle that had flown into the cellar the day he'd been born—driven in somehow by the storm. It seemed as if the sword *had* been truly meant for him. He reached out to touch the carving and cut himself on the blade, drawing blood.

Vesterkamp grunted, as if he had expected the accident to happen. "Whenever a Muramasa is fully drawn, it must taste blood. Remember this always. The sword used to belong to my own master. He felt it brought him only misfortune and gave it to me. I confess too, I'll be glad finally to be rid of it. But perhaps you are strong enough to bear the burden of carrying such a great blade."

Vesterkamp handed Nicolas a strip of cloth to bandage his wound. Nicolas wrapped the cloth around the freshly bleeding cut. "I can really keep it?"

"Yes. My parting gift to you."

"Parting? What do you mean? Surely there's more you can teach me?"

Vesterkamp seemed touched that Nicolas seemed reluctant to go, despite all that he had endured. "I've driven you hard, lad. I know how you've suffered. Most would have been eager to finish such work. But you. You still want more. You've already learned the most important thing—not to be deceived by what your eyes see. You could have chosen any of those swords. All of them are in fittings a hundred times more splendid than the Muramasa, but you looked beyond the sheath, to discover the greatness inside—just as you looked beyond what you saw of me and trusted me to teach you. There is no greater gift in swordsmanship than seeing into the true heart of things."

Vesterkamp looked straight at Nicolas, but his gaze seemed far away, as if he were walking among the visions of his past. They stared at each other for some time—master and pupil, speaking solely with their eyes. It seemed to Nicolas that Vesterkamp had opened a small window into his soul, allowing Nicolas to peer inside and share as perhaps Vesterkamp's own master had shared in turn, the deepest secrets of his school.

The communion completed the final transmission of teaching. Nicolas broke contact first, lowering his head in respectful appreciation. Vesterkamp gave Nicolas a leather harness so he could carry the sword on his back. With nothing more to say or teach, he walked back through the other room and outside into the orange light of the rising sun. Nicolas followed close behind.

Vesterkamp nodded in the direction of the harbor. "Your escort ships have arrived to take you to France. Everyone's talking about it at the port. You'd best get to the docks and be on your way back home. When you get to Paris, look up Joseph de Boulogne. Everyone knows him as the Chevalier de Saint-Georges. You've much in common, both of you. Who knows, in a few years you might even give him a run for it with the blade. Once you're in France, you should have that sword properly mounted so you can wear it on horseback. Don't entrust it to just anyone, though. Make sure they're up to the task."

Vesterkamp paused as if he'd forgotten something. He grinned at Nicolas, fixing him with his gaze. "One last thing. Have you solved the problem I posed to you on what constitutes the body of a rock?"

Nicolas shook his head. "Not yet. I confess it still doesn't make sense to me." Nicolas worried his master would be cross, but instead Vesterkamp's gaze softened, as if he were pleased there might still be something he could impart to his young prodigy.

"Try asking your friend the priest. If he doesn't know, you'll find the answer on your own in time. The riddle is part of the polishing each good sword needs to really cut. And when you do solve the puzzle, you'll then unlock the deepest insights of my style of fighting."

Nicolas extended his hand. "I'll solve it one day. I promise. I shall not forget you, nor what you have taught me. Farewell, Monsieur. I hope we shall meet again."

Vesterkamp shook with a firm grip. To Nicolas his visage remained as impenetrable as the armored mask back in his room. Before Vesterkamp could go back inside, Nicolas suddenly rushed forward and embraced him, then stepped back and mounted his horse.

"Off with you then, boy!"

*

Vesterkamp struggled to hold back the water that began to fill the corners of his eyes as he watched Nicolas doff his hat and ride away. As hard as his life had been, he felt satisfied now. All the best of him had been poured from one vessel to the other. Now he could die without feeling that the purpose of his life had been wasted.

Go on, boy. Ride off into the light of your destiny and don't look back. I've made a right mess of my own life, but you are the one thing I know I can be proud of. A part of me will carry on with you, wherever you go. With what you've learned, I pity any man foolish enough to make you his enemy.

*

Two days after leaving Ducos, Nicolas disembarked at the port of Cap Français. He left the ship and walked toward his waiting coach, tired but relieved to be on his way home. His valet Julius trailed behind him, tending to the offloading of all the trunks and baggage and the care of his mounts. Nicolas noticed two well-dressed gentlemen standing by his carriage. As he came closer, the man standing nearest to the coach turned, revealing his face in profile. Nicolas felt the thud of mischief cuff him in the gut. He knew at once, that the herald of death had dispatched its hounds, with red eyes and slavering jaws, to smell him out. Montbatre and his companion both doffed their hats in tandem, the greeting exquisitely polite, but with menace lurking just beneath the veil of courtesy.

Montbatre rose from the bow and returned his black tricorn hat to his head. "Good day to you, Monsieur d'Argentolle."

Nicolas eyed both men with guarded interest. "And to you, Monsieur Montbatre."

Nicolas knew Montbatre from the *Salon de Fer*. Montbatre's intriguing and friendliness with Mauran had gotten him expelled when Mauran disgraced himself. The other man Nicolas did not know. He seemed soft as an English pudding, with a licentious manner and a face made up with entirely too much powder and rouge to suit Nicolas' tastes. The look of well-to-do salons shaped his manners and aspect, and the scent of cheap perfume hung about his clothes, as if he'd just come straight from a brothel.

"May I present to you Monsieur le Baron de Ginestas? We are the friends of the Vidame de Saint-Dié. May we have the names of your friends?" Montbatre asked.

My friends? What manner of nonsense is this? Nicolas had heard similar words before. He knew their meaning well. Montbatre spoke the language of the duel. Mauran had dispatched these men as seconds to fix a place and time for an encounter. Nicolas faced both men down, refusing to be cowed by the implied threat of their presence. "What is the meaning of this, and what the devil is Mauran playing at? No quarrel exists between us."

Montbatre sniffed the air with nervousness, shifting his weight from one foot to the other, unable to keep still. "He plays at nothing, Monsieur le Chevalier. He is the gentleman

158

whose honor you sullied at the *Salon de Fer*. After a match in which you defeated him with a dishonorable ploy, you then proceeded to add further injury to his honor by commenting to others he lacked skill enough to contest with you, when you knew only illness on the day prevented him from being at his best."

Nicolas regarded Montbatre with derision, incensed he should be drawn into an affair of honor on such a blatantly manufactured pretext. "What I remember, Monsieur, is I had the pleasure of contesting with the vidame in a special bout before the entire salon. I recorded sixteen touches and he recorded none. After the sixteenth, he excused himself on the pretext of taking a piss and instead took a pisser. As to all else you allege, it is complete and utter nonsense. If your friend, however, is determined to add another setback to his long record of ignominy, I shall of course be happy to oblige him."

"Your friends, Monsieur?" the Baron de Ginestas whined, his lips puckering obscenely as he spoke.

"I would not ask my donkey to stand up in such a farce. But as it seems you are determined to carry on, you may speak with the Comte de Marbéville, who will act for me. Now, gentlemen, I bid you good day."

Nicolas tipped his hat in the barest manner of civility as his valet Julius came up with his baggage. Mauran's seconds removed their hats, bowing as courtesy demanded. Nicolas ignored them and entered his coach.

Damn that fool, Mauran. What could he be up to? He's no match for me and he knows it, and I never made such a ridiculous comment as he alleged. I'll have to have Francis insist on blades, as this smells of another's influence. But who would put him up to such a thing? As soon as Julius got inside, Nicolas ordered the driver to set off.

*

The Baron de Ginestas removed his hat and fanned himself against the heat as Nicolas' coach pulled away. "Excellent, Montbatre, how well you played your part. You should take up acting as a side profession."

Montbatre smiled at the compliment. He liked praise almost as much as he liked money. "You think he took the bait?"

The baron nodded in approval. "Swallowed it whole. He's certain to be suspicious, and he's clever enough to ensure pistols won't be used, which will unwittingly play right into our hands. The chevalier knows Mauran's no match for him, so he'll be confident of his victory, but he doesn't know his adversary's blade will be poisoned, and just the lightest of touches will result in certain death. It's a pity, you know, he's even more beautiful than I'd heard. What a delight it would be to take him as a lover, but we're being well-paid to put an end to him, and put an end to him we shall."

Ginestas' voice had an odd timbre, part whine, part wheeze. Montbatre took a pinch of snuff from an ornate snuffbox, sneezing several times into his handkerchief. "You can bugger him when he's dead, as long as I get my share of what's coming to me, Baron. We'll need to do the thing quickly, though, before their ships sail for France."

Ginestas returned his hat to his head. "A costume ball will be held at the Montferraud estate in a few days. All the elite society of the island will be there. It'll be the perfect time to stage the duel. I know the place well enough. There's a secluded clearing behind the outermost stable wall, which would suit our purpose exceedingly well. You shall prepare it with torches and the other necessary requirements. I shall confront him at the fête and bring him to the location. Make sure you train Mauran with diligence. He needs to be capable enough to at least nick the fellow. The poison is slow-acting so the chevalier should be aboard ship and well-away from here before it begins to take real effect. With any luck he'll be buried at sea, which will conveniently absolve us of any blame, and avoid the added inconvenience of a body to examine."

Montbatre nodded his head in appreciation. "Damned clever. Who wants him dead so badly they're willing to go to such lengths? He seems a fine enough fellow to me."

"Never you mind, sweet Montbatre. You have done your work well in infiltrating the salon, stirring up trouble and recruiting Mauran to play the part of the fool. I am of course, wholly relying upon your judgment that the pawn's skill is sufficient to carry out the task we require of him."

Montbatre nodded. "I've been giving the vidame some special lessons of late. He's much better than when he left the salon. Good enough to do the job reliably, and he is eager to redeem his reputation. He just needs a little confidence and I'm sure he'll stick the bastard at least once. And if he doesn't, I'll nick the chevalier myself 'by accident' when he's unawares."

"Good. I'm sure your poisonous whispers helped nurture the seed of enmity which envy had already planted in the vidame's heart. Have you sent the letter to the marquis as I told you to?"

"Delivered yesterday, Baron."

Ginestas grinned a wicked smile. "Excellent. Now we watch and wait. Just be grateful there is no business more lucrative or constant than death, Montbatre, and we, thankfully, are to be the happy and fruitful purveyors of it."

Scent of the Black Flower

Nicolas noticed the change as soon as his carriage approached the gate to the outer courtyard of the Blaise estate in Caracol. The usual attendants keeping watch over the approaches to the château complex had been reinforced. Seven men formed the normal guard contingent; three posted by the main gate supported by a pair of watchers for each side entrance. But as he passed through the outer gate, he saw at least a dozen men, four by the main gate and twice that number fanned out along the approach, all armed with muskets and pistols. Many faces were new to him. He sat up straight to observe as the men waved him through into the lower courtyard. More men were inside. Some patrolling the walls and others standing on alert. It seemed to Nicolas that his home had been transformed into an armed camp, and he wondered what had occurred to effectuate such a change.

The coach passed through the inner courtyard and approached the main entrance stairs. Nicolas got down in front of the familiar marble steps and turned to look back before going inside. On the roofs of the stables and the courtyard outbuildings stood two teams of sharpshooters, one on each side. One of the men tipped his hat to Nicolas. Nicolas returned the courtesy.

"What has happened while I've been away?" Nicolas asked of no one in particular. He took the Muramasa from the coach as Julius took charge of arranging the unloading and transport of the baggage. Nicolas slung the sword across his back then turned and went inside. A pair of lackeys held the doors open for him as he crossed into the vestibule.

Once inside, Nicolas handed the long sword to his valet, along with his hat, travelling gloves and cloak. "Take this to my room and store it within reach of the bed till I can have a proper stand made for it."

Julius bowed and headed off toward the family rooms. Nicolas went in search of his mother, drawn in by the sounds of a harpsichord. He went to the music room and found the marquise practicing a prelude by Couperin, her back toward the door. Nicolas crept forward and planted a kiss on his mother's cheek. Madame de Blaise turned with a start, then rose and threw her arms about her son's neck.

"My dearest child, we hadn't expected you back for another day or so."

Nicolas sat on the harpsichord bench next to his mother, one arm around her waist, the other eyeing the pages of the music she played. "You have favorable winds and a fast coach to thank for my early arrival, Maman. Your playing has improved since I left. This piece is quite difficult, but you've managed it very well. I heard you from the hall."

Madame de Blaise smiled at the words of praise and returned to her playing. "I'm glad you noticed, my dear. I've been working quite faithfully at my lessons while you were away on Martinique. I find it helps the idle time to pass and I shall soon have many empty hours in need of useful employment. I prefer music rather than melancholy to fill them."

Nicolas began turning the pages. He waited for his mother to say more, but she finished her thoughts only with Couperin's intricate melody. Nicolas frowned as he considered how to broach the subject of all the new faces at the château. He wondered if his mother's remark and the new men guarding the house were related?

The marquise glanced at Nicolas and halted her playing. She stroked Nicolas' brow to brighten his expression, then took his large hand in hers and kissed it. "It wasn't so long ago, I used to hold you on my lap so you could peck at the keys. It used to delight you so. How long has it been since you last played?"

"A long time, Maman. Not with any regularity since I returned from Brienne."

The marquise gave Nicolas a gently admonishing gaze. "You have a gift for music, my dear heart. Just like your father. You shouldn't give it up. I tell him the same thing as well. One of these days I'm determined to hear you both play together."

Nicolas grinned. "I haven't given it up, Maman. I suppose I'm like Papa in that I prefer not to play than to play badly, and I haven't been diligent enough to keep up my practice. I believe I can still do justice to this fine instrument, though."

Madame de Blaise tugged Nicolas' hand toward the keys. "Good, then you can do this part for me. I find it too difficult at the proper tempo."

Nicolas grinned at his mother. "I know you can really do it, Maman, but I'm pleased to play for you, nonetheless."

Nicolas breezed through the remainder of the prelude from memory as the marquise listened beside him. He didn't miss a note. When he finished, Madame de Blaise bestowed kisses to each cheek as reward. "Thank you, dear child. You still play beautifully. It gives me great pleasure to hear you again, and to see how big and strong you've become. Why your hands make mine look so small now."

The marquise placed her hands on top of Nicolas' for comparison, delighted to let her son bask in the warmth of her warmth and praise. "But as glorious as you always seem to me, you do look tired. I hope you haven't pushed yourself too hard."

Nicolas leaned over and kissed his mother's cheek. "I must force myself on if I am to be worthy of the prize I seek, Maman."

The marquise smiled back with indulgence. "I grant you your prize is very sweet and more than a little adorable. Don't worry my son, she's missed you as much as you've missed her, perhaps more. She told me so in her letters."

Nicolas regarded his mother with surprise. Though glad to know he'd been missed, he seemed unsure of what to make of his mother's separate correspondence with Sérolène.

"You've exchanged letters with Mademoiselle de La Bouhaire, Maman?"

The marquise tugged at Nicolas' dimpled cheek then kissed him gently on the lips. A habit of affection she'd engaged in since she had cradled him as a baby. "Why of course I have, my dear. Like every girl hopelessly in love, she wants to know everything about you, and who could possibly know more about you than your own Maman? You needn't look so concerned my love, I've no need to pry. A mother understands these things and knows what's best. Besides, she tells me everything in any case."

"Maman!" Nicolas exclaimed.

"Oh, Maman yourself. Of course she should confide in me. Whom else should she trust to ensure her happiness? Do

166

you expect she should leave such an important thing up to her aunt, or to you men? Why, the lot of you would bungle things beyond salvaging. Now you may leave me in peace. I must practice more before my lesson tomorrow. Kiss me again, my beautiful boy, then go and see your father. He's been so busy with all his plans as of late, he scarcely has time for any of us. I'm sure he'll be happy to see you, though. He's in his study."

The marquise resumed her playing. Nicolas left her with a parting gift of several more kisses to her cheek, and then went off in search of his father. He found the marquis in the study as his mother foretold, surrounded by several secretaries and even more stacks of papers and correspondence. The marquis glanced briefly at Nicolas, but remained behind his desk, too busy to spare the time for a proper greeting. Nicolas thought his father looked unusually harried and more than a little tired.

The marquis beckoned Nicolas forward as a clerk placed a document for his signature on the desk. He began to read it as he spoke, looking at the document and not at Nicolas. "Well, Monsieur, you are back, and a day early, it seems. Monsignor Arnaud tells me he is satisfied with your progress. Apparently, you devoured mathematics and the sciences in the same manner as languages and history. He keeps trying to change my mind about the decision to send you to the École Militaire, but that bridge has already been crossed and soon we shall burn it entirely. Has all of your baggage arrived as well? Most of it might as well remain in your trunks. It'll spare the effort of having to pack it twice."

After three months of hard toil away from his family, Nicolas stiffened at receiving so indifferent a greeting from the man whose approval meant more to him than anything in the world. "It has, Monsieur le Marquis, and of course I shall arrange my baggage however you should like. Will that be all?"

*

The marquis looked up from the document, reacting at once to the unaccustomed tone of petulance in his son's voice. The boy he expected to see standing there, however, had disappeared. Before him stood a young man much matured from the one he'd sent away. *How swiftly time passes. When did the lad I jostled on my knee grow into such a fine man? Where has that sweet little child gone?*

The marquis dismissed the others from the room. Once they were gone, he walked to the other side of the desk and embraced Nicolas. Holding him at arm's length, he squeezed his son's muscular torso and shoulders until the chevalier grinned, revealing both his dimples.

"So, you've been busy it seems. Your ordeal has given you a new physique to prove it. I know you've worked hard, but you'll find such efforts worth the sacrifice. Your new studies will prepare you well for Paris. I expect much from you, Nicolas."

Nicolas nodded. "I'll not let you down, Papa."

The marquis allowed his thoughts to drift away from the cryptic anonymous note delivered to him the day before. A dispatch with just one symbol drawn upon a single page. A black fleur-de-lis. "You've never disappointed me. You have always been the best of sons, but as strong and capable as you have been, I need you to be even stronger. There is much now at stake. My enemies know I mean to return to France and they've sent me their warning to stay put. This time I shall defy them, come what may for all of us. I trust you've noticed the many new faces about the château and grounds?"

"Yes, Papa. It looks like a small army. May I ask who they are and why they're here?"

"The new men are here to protect us, and more will join them soon. I shall have to rely on them all to keep the family safe until we depart. Once we are in Paris, the people of the city will defend us. My enemies will try and strike before we arrive, but they will find we are better armored than they had planned for."

The marquis began to pace across the study, usually a clue to those who knew him that he had something important and perhaps also lengthy, to say. "It pleases me, Nicolas that you and Francis are close, but as first born, your brother has the advantage of seniority and the privileges which go with it. He has come to rely on them, while you've had to trust in your own talents. You've studied history, and read of the fall of the empires of old. Well, we're the old empire now, and we have our own similar problems to solve. Fortunately, we have the example of the Americans to guide us, and we must not mistake the meaning of what they strive to accomplish."

The marquis stopped pacing to look directly at his son. "I want you to understand why I work so hard, Nicolas. The baron and I are joining with others to build a new future, one that will be more open to men of talent, regardless of birth. Men like you will flourish in our new world, but the transformation may prove to be more of a struggle than Francis expects. You have no golden chains to hold you back. Your future shall be what you decide to make of it. Therein lies both blessing and curse."

Nicolas listened in silence as the marquis resumed his pacing. "It's important you do well at your studies, and that you support your brother as much as you are able to from now on. I have given Francis the means to sustain himself and his family, at least for the near future. Of course he will also inherit the rest of my estates and fortune when I die."

"Please, Father. It's too early to talk of such a thing."

The marquis looked toward the drawer, which concealed the letter of warning. "I hope to have many years left to see my grandchildren; both your brother's and yours. However, we must prepare for all eventualities. Therefore, Nicolas, I leave you the least but also the best and the hardest thing I can…the necessity and the opportunity for you to rise in the world on your own merit. My exile from the court did not ruin me. On the contrary, it made me stronger. You must also find a way to turn adversity to advantage. Your estates will provide you a suitable income for a beginning. The rest, you must do on your own. Francis hasn't your strength. He will require yours in support. You, for your part, can make use of his advice, his influence, and his alliances. The times before us will be turbulent ones. You will both need each other."

"I understand. I promise I will do my best to help Francis."

Blaise returned to sit at his desk. "Well, what more could a father ask of a son? I have other news of interest, which concerns you, though before you receive it, I forbid you to mention it to anyone. Do you accept my condition?"

The marquis waited until Nicolas nodded his assent before continuing. "I've made another decision on your behalf while you were away—without your knowledge, it is true, but I'm assured by your mother it will not disappoint you."

The marquis saw Nicolas shift his feet with anxiety as he waited for further explanation. "Whatever it is, Papa, I'm sure it's for the best."

"Very well, then. Before you left for Martinique, Baron Salvagnac approached me to discuss the matter of your relationship with the Vicomtesse de La Bouhaire. As I told you before, we agreed you would be allowed to pay formal court to the vicomtesse."

Nicolas shifted nervously as his father's eyes bored into him. The marquis gave his son a half smile to ease his nerves. "Since the conclusion of that agreement, the baron and I have spoken about the same matter at length, and on several occasions. Suffice it to say we aired our differing perspectives, and in order to bolster your suit, I added the lands of Cerneaux and Blinfey to your existing domains, which more than doubles your current income. I am told by your sister Julienne, that my actions had an immediate and salutary effect upon Madame de Salvagnac, as I suspected they would. Your new lands and income impressed the baron suitably enough for him to agree in principle to your betrothal to his niece. You are to be married when the vicomtesse is seventeen and of age, provided she will still have you when the time comes."

Nicolas stared at the marquis in dumbfounded silence. His mouth hung open but he made no sound. The marquis gave a wry smile. "I assume by your silence you have no objections to my arrangements?"

Nicolas rushed to kneel and kiss his father's hand. "Father...it's more than I had ever dared hope for."

"Rise up, my boy. I'm *your* father, not the Holy Father. Besides, it is your doing, not mine. You have so endeared the young lady to you she will have no other. I do not wish to sound cruel, but I caution you she is still young, and hearts have been known to change. You must wait almost two years before she can marry. Time will pass quickly, although I know it must seem like a lifetime to you now. Use the interval well, so when the day comes, you will both be ready."

"Does she know? The vicomtesse, I mean," Nicolas asked.

Blaise shook his head. "Under the law she must give her consent freely in order for your betrothal to be recognized as valid and legally binding. The baron has vouchsafed this consent exists on her behalf, but she may later undo it if she so chooses, so we deemed it best to keep the matter confidential from her for now."

"I understand. Thank you, Papa! You have given me more than I'd ever dared to dream!"

The marquis frowned. He placed both arms behind his back in contemplation. "Very well, then. You've plenty of work yet to do before we depart. I've received word our ships are ready to sail. It will only be a matter of days now before we leave. Madame de Blaise will not be sailing with us. I know you will regret her temporary loss as much as I, but I believe it in the best interests of all for her arrival in France to be delayed."

Nicolas gave the marquis a look of forlorn understanding. "Ah, so that's why Maman has been so diligent with her practice habits. She's hoping to give herself something to do once we depart. But must she really remain here alone, Father? I shall miss her most dreadfully, but I imagine she'll also be very lonely with everyone gone. It's almost like she's being abandoned."

Blaise sighed deeply. "Regrettably, things are not always as easy or as straightforward as they might seem. You have not known how deeply she suffered after we first married. Some of the things whispered about us were vile and abominable. In the more disreputable parts of Cap Français, they even made crude drawings of us on the walls. In those days, I never allowed her to go out into the city without a sizeable retinue of escorts—both for her own safety, and to make sure she never saw any of those wretched scribbles."

Nicolas glanced at his father, the marquise saw the light of understanding begin to dawn in his son's eyes. "I have exactly seven wounds on my body, Nicolas, but in all my years with the cavalry I never took one wound while serving with the regiment. All of my injuries came from the duels I fought against those who slandered your mother. I don't regret a single one of them. They were a small price to pay for sending a dozen scoundrels to their graves."

The marquis saw the shock on Nicolas' face. "You look surprised. Well, don't be. The training you received had a very real and immediate purpose. I want you to be as prepared as you can be for what you might also face. There are those who will resent greatly my return to France. I have already received a letter from Montbarrey to be watchful for my safety. Many old debts will come due over the coming months, my boy. Some will prove easier to collect than others. Both you and Francis must be on your guard. I don't know when or how my enemies will choose to strike at me, but strike they will, perhaps even through one of you. In order to ensure your mother remains safe, I have chosen to have her remain here until I send for her."

"Do you think things will be as bad in Paris for Maman? Won't she find a safer home in such an enlightened city? Great writers and thinkers like Voltaire are welcomed in its streets and salons…"

The marquis' face darkened. "Among men of letters Voltaire may indeed be a giant, but when it comes to certain subjects, you will find how quickly he shrinks, till he is no bigger than a circus dwarf. Read his works and you'll discover my meaning for yourself. He had the temerity to affront me once with an insolent letter concerning your mother's origins. I had him beaten within an inch of his life. When he recovered, he fled Paris in fear."

Nicolas regarded his father with surprise. "And you escaped any punishment or censure, Father?"

Blaise folded his arms across his chest. "I was not the only one he had annoyed, just the most willing to do something about it. Had he been my equal, I'd have called him out. As it happened, the King took my side of it and banished the scribbler from court. I know this is all rather new to you, Nicolas. Both your mother and I hoped to spare you from as much of the unwelcome past as we could. But you are a man now, and need to prepare for what lies ahead of you. I confess I'd not presumed you would become attached so young. I believed we would have more time before we needed to concern ourselves with such matters, but here we are, nevertheless."

Nicolas bowed his head in thought. "Yes, Father. Here we are nonetheless."

The marquis stopped pacing to look directly at his son. "Some of those whose family members I sent onward are still at court. They will not have forgotten nor forgiven what transpired, even though matters occurred long ago. The influence of my enemies has increased over time, given their nearness to our sovereign. But the hubris of their ill-gotten power will cause them to overreach. When they do, we will take advantage. Because these old feuds are governed by the strictures of the Code Duello—the code of the duel—we cannot act against each other publicly. But this offers less protection than it seems, for it means only that they will act through proxies. Be assured, Nicolas, our enemies will be waiting with snares aplenty to entrap all of us should we falter, your mother especially. I won't allow her to be hurt, or ridiculed or slandered. The way must be adequately prepared before she arrives. Do you understand?"

Nicolas nodded. "I do, Papa. But when do you think she might join us?"

"I shall send for your mother once things are settled enough so her arrival both in Paris and at court will not cause the worst of the old quarrels to be reopened. Precisely when, though, I cannot say. I should be very much obliged if you could make an effort to spend time with her before we depart. She'll be on her own once we set sail, as the Salvagnacs will also be sailing with us. I know it's disappointing. Rest assured, no one will miss her more than I, but regretfully, this is the way it must be."

Nicolas lowered his head with resignation. "I understand, Father."

"That reminds me. We will be having a special event here a few days from now. I suppose you could call it our farewell party. It'll be a costume affair, so see to it you have something suitable. The place will be full of the best society of the island, including one particular vicomtesse whom I believe you're rather fond of."

Nicolas beamed at the news. "Sérolène, I mean, Mademoiselle de La Bouhaire, will be here?"

"Yes, of course, along with the rest of the Salvagnacs and two hundred or so others. There is nothing more disconcerting to your enemies than appearing wholly indifferent to their threats and posturing. By opening our house with such boldness, we show everyone we cannot be cowed. I expect it will please you very much to be reunited with your La Bouhaire after so long a separation. I wonder if she'll still recognize you, you've changed so."

"I shall be very glad to see her again, Papa. But if everyone is in costume, how will I know her?"

"Ask your mother. She's developed quite a correspondence with the vicomtesse while you were away. If anyone knows what her costume will be, your mother will know. Now off with you, Monsieur. I've still some matters to attend to here. Remember, I expect the best from you. Let nothing stand in your way."

*

Nicolas embraced his father once more, then turned and left the room. *Betrothed to Sérolène!* He felt light as a feather, and wanted to run and shout his elation to the entire world! But the thought of being absent from his mother, dampened the mood of celebration. He went to his room and sat down upon the bed. His father's words still echoed in his ears. *We are building a new future, one more open to men of talent, regardless of birth.*

Once they arrived in France, Sérolène might draw the attention of many in search of a pretty wife and a large dowry, though on the latter point it seemed he had little reason to fear, as the vicomtesse had no fortune of her own. She had mentioned to him many times, that she lived on the charity of her relatives. But Nicolas didn't care if she hadn't a sou to her name. He loved her, and had more than enough for the both to them to live on in comfort.

Julius entered the room with a tray full of refreshments and Nicolas suddenly remembered the visit from Mauran's seconds. The sword of honor had but a single point, but many facets to its blade. Some darker than others. He got to his feet.

"Julius, I must go and speak to Francis about being my second. It's a damned stupid thing, but it must be settled before we leave for France. I shall also have to procure an outfit for the upcoming fête. Tomorrow we'll go into town and see about a suitable costume. I have something both simple and extravagant in mind, but we shall see what can be done with just a day or two to prepare. Wait here for me till I return."

Julius set down the tray. "As you will, Monseigneur."

Nicolas left the room to find his brother. First, he would fulfill the obligations to his honor. Then he would conjure up a costume splendid enough to catch the eye and the heart of a very special vicomtesse. He grinned to himself, and gave a tribute to fortune for procuring for him an angel who walked the earth. One to whom he was now secretly and most happily betrothed.

Deception

A palpable hum of excitement buzzed about the guests as they began arriving at the Blaise estate, the courtyard and surrounding grounds already filling with carriages as the sun descended into the verdant hillside. Along the entire length of the road from the border of the plantation to the château itself, lanterns hung from the branches of trees. Half a mile from the outer courtyard, stakes driven into the ground at regular intervals, held torches pitched atop them, providing a gleaming pathway of light to guide the arriving carriages.

The Salvagnac coach pulled into the main courtyard, disgorging its passengers into the reception line, which snaked out the front door well past the marble entrance steps. Sérolène waited eagerly in line, bursting with anticipation to see Nicolas. For her costume, she had chosen a golden gown of the more loosely flowing style known as *volante*, which had been popular in the early part of the century. She wore her hair dressed in a high coiffure known as Lilac, which had its basic heart shape teased wider and augmented with wire framed silk attachments to represent a glowing sun. A golden mask carved in the shape of a butterfly, extended from the top of her forehead to the crest of her upper lip. Because of her great height, further augmented by more than a foot of hair, those who knew her might divine her identity at first sight. But Sérolène gave not thought to hiding in plain sight. She *wanted* to be seen, and to look as resplendent as she felt. Tonight she would lay eyes on the man she loved again after months of being apart, and her heart sang in anticipation.

The vicomtesse waited with Éléonore in the midst of the receiving line, just behind the Baron and Baronne de Salvagnac. Her aunt and uncle, along with her young *cousine*, were dressed as characters from the Beaumarchais play *Le Barbier de Séville ou la Précaution inutile*. The baron came as Count Almaviva, sporting a flamboyant Spanish costume complete with cape, and mask with moustache attached. The baronne came as Rosine, in a bright red *robe à la française* adorned with large colorful butterflies. She wore an ornate butterfly mask to conceal her identity. Éléonore wore a bright red Harlequin costume and mask, representing the barber, Figaro. It took but a few excited moments for them to pass through a gauntlet of welcoming footmen all dressed in uniform similar to the Royal Swiss Guards, and enter the sumptuously decorated entranceway framed with floral garlands and ribbons in a variety of colors.

Once inside, the queue of new arrivals still extended well past the vestibule, making for a wait of several more minutes before they reached the head of the receiving line. Waiting to greet them stood Julienne, Francis, and the marquis. Julienne wore an elaborate shepherdess costume of white, her hair done up in a powdered Charlotte[x] coiffure with a very large bow at the top. She carried a long staff in her right hand, with a white and green bow attached just under the hook, to symbolize her recent marriage. Francis wore a Turkish outfit, with wide red pantaloons, a green vest, a red and yellow striped silk robe and a fanciful yellow turban atop his head trimmed in scarlet. The marquis dressed as a Tartar horseman, with light pink long jacket, baggy green pantaloons, high leather boots and red and green high turban cap. None of the welcoming party wore their masks, since their duties as hosts called for them to greet and welcome all the arriving guests.

The marquis recognized the vicomtesse at once, and pulled Sérolène aside to speak a quiet word with her. "You look splendid, my dear vicomtesse. Your gown takes me back to my own youth. Look for another golden princess, and keep an eye out for Greeks bearing gifts."

The marquis returned to exchange extended greetings with the rest of the Salvagnacs, who then entered the main salon to mingle with the other guests. Sérolène exchanged final kisses with Julienne before hurrying to catch up with her aunt and uncle, who stood in the midst of the crowded *salon de compagnie* with Éléonore. As she tried to make her way forward, Sérolène yielded right of passage to a couple garbed as peacocks complete with plumage, who strolled across her path. When the way cleared again to move forward, Sérolène had lost sight of her uncle and aunt in the press of the crowd. As she turned to backtrack toward the vestibule, a woman dressed in a magnificent *grand habit*—a formal gown of golden silk brocade—approached and entwined her arm with Sérolène's own. Not even the lady's ornate golden mask, crafted to resemble Vesta, the Roman goddess of hearth and family, could completely hide her beauty or her striking green eyes.

Sérolène embraced the marquise in delight. "Madame de Blaise! I missed you in the receiving line and wondered where you might be. Oh, how I wish I would grow up to be as beautiful as you are!"

The marquise returned the embrace. "You do know how to make a woman feel appreciated, my dear child. Come with me. I have a surprise for you."

*

The marquise led Sérolène through the salon and out into the rear promenade and courtyard, which extended the full length of the château and opened into the gardens. The château and its grounds overflowed with revelers—talking, dancing, and sampling a variety of dishes from liveried servants, who passed by with silver plates piled high with delicacies. Other lackeys circulated amongst the crowd with trays of crystal glasses offering champagne, wine, and ale to the guests. For the few who drank no spirits and younger attendees, a variety of sweetened juices made from oranges, mangoes, and lemons also circulated on trays. A large section of the garden lay cordoned off for dancing, the orchestra already busily engaged. The usual staff of household servants had also been augmented with more than two dozen men dressed as Swiss Guards, who stood watch at all the key doors and entrances to ensure the security of the house. They were the marquis' private protectors, an insurance policy against anyone attempting to use the crowd and the convenience of costume as a cover to strike at the family.

Madame de Blaise took Sérolène by the hand as they walked. "I've told Solomon to inform the baronne I've borrowed you for a little while, and you shall be under my tutelage tonight. Come, let's chat while we walk. Your letters have kept me informed on how you've been faring, but I do so want to hear more about the particulars, since I now have some time with you in person."

Sérolène opened up to Madame de Blaise with eagerness, filling her in on the many small but important things that had happened since they last met. They walked past a group of gentlemen, who were not content to appreciate their passing in silence but chose to favor both ladies with loud declarations of admiration. Sérolène blushed beneath her mask and turned her head away from the costumed revelers.

Madame de Blaise sensed the vicomtesse's unease, and placed a reassuring arm around Sérolène's waist. "You must not let such notice disturb you, my dear. That is what they wish. Besides, I am sure such attention will only increase, as you grow older. You're becoming quite a beauty, you know."

Sérolène flushed with pride, which displayed itself as a gentle deepening of pink along the nape of her long slender neck. "Thank you, Madame. Do you think Monsieur d'Argentolle will find me pleasing enough?"

They halted beneath one of the many lanterns that hung in the gardens, bathing the area with light. Madame de Blaise took Sérolène's hands and held them. "I hope, dear child, you do not doubt either the degree or the sincerity of my son's affections."

"Oh, no, Madame! I didn't mean to imply that at all. I just haven't seen him in some time and I hope he finds me…I mean my costume…to his liking."

The marquise gave Sérolène a reassuring hug, pausing to admire the vicomtesse's perfectly worn *volante* of yellow-gold. The style exuded the elegance of a bygone era when France stood both proud *and* prosperous. Among the many other ladies in attendance, no other guest had transformed her attire into a symbol of glamour in the manner of the vicomtesse. On her, it seemed not merely a costume, but a harbinger of her future place, of the greatness still to come. The marquise noticed how heads turned as they passed. She suspected the sight of the vicomtesse set more than a few pulses racing, and not just because she towered over most of the crowd.

Madame de Blaise leaned close to make herself heard over the din of the orchestra playing for the dancers in the courtyard. "How could he not be? You're absolutely stunning, my dear, and rest assured, he's talked of nothing but you all day. But don't tell him I told you so."

Sérolène's contented smile gave the marquise all the reply needed. The pair continued to walk arm in arm past the dense throng of the island's elite. On every side, there were diversions set up to entertain the guests; cards, billiards, games of wit, and conversation. And for those in search of passive diversion, there were jugglers, circus players, and two troops of actors to provide entertainment.

Madame de Blaise passed through two guards and entered the private entrance to the west wing of the château, to which only the family had access. They climbed up to the second story and the marquise showed Sérolène into a private library. The library ran nearly thirty feet in length and twenty in width, with an attached hearth and a separate reading room to the left of the central fireplace. This smaller room, paneled in mahogany, contained a day bed, four large reading chairs, and a desk in one corner. Bookshelves covered the length of all the walls, extending from floor to ceiling. A fire burned in the hearth, giving the library an aura of calm amidst the general commotion outside and below. Nicolas' valet, Julius, stood in attendance by the door to the reading room.

Julius bowed low as the marquise and Sérolène entered. The marquise directed Sérolène to enter and then planted a motherly kiss, on the vicomtesse's gold-masked forehead. "Happy belated birthday, my child. Your host awaits you inside. Julius will tend to any needs you might have."

*

The marquise left to rejoin the party. Julius indicated to Sérolène to pass through the open door to his right, on the far side of the hearth. Sérolène crossed the room and went through the opening. She entered a short corridor lined with more books. She pulled in her skirts to avoid them knocking into the cabinets and objects on sconces along the walls and turned right into another room the size of a large parlor, paneled entirely in mahogany and walnut. The room contained a small dining table, a chaise longue and a second hearth. The hearth's position lay reversed to the one in the main room. In front of the hearth stood a long sofa. A man stood at the far end of the room, his broad back leaning against one of the bookshelves.

The vicomtesse stopped just inside the door. The figure looked magnificent, garbed in the battle costume of Alexander the Great, complete with plumed helmet, cloak, and greaves. The wearer sported a Greek-styled white linen tunic trimmed with red and gold, over which he wore a detailed chest piece carved with lion figures. A bronze lion's head clasp at the shoulder, secured a crimson knee-length cloak in place. The warrior's feet, adorned with calf-high leather boots, bleached to match the tunic, revealed the rippling muscles of his legs in their natural state, without breeches or tights to cover them; a shockingly bold statement by the wearer. Atop his head sat a faithful replica of the great man's famous lion-head helmet, complete with a red central plume and two long white feathers protruding upwards from the front like antlers.

Sérolène's pulse quickened with admiration and also doubt. Yes, her Nicolas was strong, but the man before her had the chiseled body of Hercules. For a brief moment, she questioned who it might be, but once he cast his gaze upon her, she knew his identity with certainty. No one else in the world had jewels for eyes, nor any as fine, green, and sparkling as the ones watching her from behind the helmet. The warrior removed his helm, welcoming her with open arms and a grin that flashed twin sparkling dimples.

Sérolène rushed forward with a squeal of delight and fell into her beloved's embrace. "Nicolas!"

She threw off her mask and pressed her lips against his. Her tongue forced an opening past his lips, which were still gentle and shy. Hers starved with want for him and boldly took their fill. He kissed her back, until she drank enough of him to let just her gaze drink him in.

"Well, my princess, I understood you to have little love for dusty antiquity. I would have long ago adopted the costume of Alexander, had I known it would uncover so swift a path to your heart."

Sérolène wrapped her arms around Nicolas' broad torso and pressed him close. "It is not the costume I love, but the wearer of it. Even in your helmet, I knew you. Your matchless eyes gave you away, and Monsieur de Blaise warned me to be on the lookout for Greeks."

Nicolas stroked Sérolène's cheek. She felt the rock of his body mold her softer flesh through her garments. She wondered if the sensation felt as good to him as it did to her, then saw the longing in his gaze and guessed that it must be so.

He took her hand and kissed it. "Since we first met in your uncle's library, I considered it fitting to arrange something for you in this favorite library of mine."

Before he could say more, Sérolène silenced him with another kiss, this one taken at a much more leisurely pace than the first. When it finally came to a sweet, bitter end, Nicolas had reached behind his back to present Sérolène with a brightly wrapped package.

"This Greek also bears thee a gift. But have no fear, my glorious Helen. There are no Trojans inside. At least none to do you harm."

Sérolène took the gift in one hand. With the other, she led Nicolas to a nearby sofa and bid him sit beside her as she unwrapped it. Inside the sheaf of red and gold wrapping, she uncovered a richly bound book of poems by Racine.

"Oh, how sweet and thoughtful of you, Nicolas!"

She opened the cover. On the jacket cover Nicolas had written her a note in Greek. A note expressing his ardent love and devotion.

Για πιο αγαπητούς μου αγάπη. Η ανάσα της ζωής μου, ο παλμός της καρδιάς μου, το φως της ψυχής μου. Για πάντα.[xi]

Sérolène traced the flowing script with her fingers as she slowly read the dedication, caressing the ink as if it were the sender's own skin.

"Happy birthday, Séro. I know it is well past January, but the circumstances of my departure prevented me from giving it to you on your real birthday. I hope you'll forgive the very belated nature of the gift. You know how much I love tragedies, so I couldn't resist something from Racine. I believe you'll find many matters of the heart to occupy you between its covers. I shall never forget the wisdom you imparted to me on the subject when we first met."

Sérolène leaned her head on Nicolas' shoulder. "Such beautiful words, Nico. I promise I'll try very hard to deserve them. Thank you, my love. I shall treasure it always."

Sérolène lifted her chin toward Nicolas and closed her eyes. She felt his lips press down upon her own. The scent and feel of him intoxicated her. The taste of him in her mouth like sweet wine, strong and pungent. Could heaven itself exceed the bliss of just one of his kisses?

After a languid, splendid eternity, Sérolène drew back, cradling her head against Nicolas' huge chest. "I love you so much, Nico."

He took her chin in his hand. "I missed you so much these past months. The best part of my day came in reading your letters. My father told me you and the Salvagnacs shall be joining us in Paris. I don't usually look forward to being so long at sea, but the idea of spending several weeks in your company makes the prospect much more inviting. Perhaps when we reach France, I can persuade your uncle to let you come to Argentolle with your governess and perhaps my brother and sister, as well. My father added the lands near Cerneaux and the woods surrounding Blinfey to my estates and I'd like you to see them. I passed through there once in my youth but have no real remembrance of what they are like. I'd hoped we might be able to discover them together."

Sérolène warmed with excitement to the proposition of seeing Nicolas' domains. "I'm so excited Nico. Ever since my uncle told me about the voyage I could hardly wait to depart. I haven't been back to France since I came here as a small child. Oh, how I would love to accompany you to your lands. What more do you know of them? Is your château large or small? Please tell me all you can. You mustn't leave out any detail!"

Nicolas grinned at Sérolène's enthusiasm. "I know precious little, really. I had only the briefest chance to visit Argentolle when I attended Brienne. It seemed well situated, and the lands provide a very comfortable income. The domain includes a small village, some nice woods plentiful with game, and a tolerable manor house, though Francis deems it more of a hunting lodge, and not a very grand one. I don't know much about the area near Cerneaux, but my new lands near Blinfey are extensively forested and ideal for game. Perhaps one day we might decide to make some changes to render the whole of it more accommodating; in whatever direction your tastes are inclined, of course."

Sérolène warmed at the prospect of being mistress of so large an estate. In her joy, she rose, coaxing Nicolas into an impromptu dance as the strains from a rondo wafted up from the floor beneath them.

Sérolène spun around, laughing with delight. "I should very much like to see our little lodge, Nico."

At the second turn, when they were meant to arc away from each other, she turned toward him instead, kissing him again on the lips.

"Séro..."

Sérolène looked up at Nicolas, her visage woozy with adoration as the sound of her name rumbled up from deep within his chest. She loved the way he called her; part sigh, part groan, a mixture of prayer and lamentation. She squeezed Nicolas' large hands in her own, her lips parting in a grin.

"I've been reading up on romantic things...can you tell? I found a pamphlet in Maria's quarters. She's my aunt's handmaid. Such a badly written thing, pictures mostly...but it contained an entire chapter on kissing. Can you believe it, a whole chapter? I decided to practice some of what it said...so I could surprise you, but I had only my pillow as a stand-in. Did I do it the wrong way earlier? Do you not like kissing me?"

Sérolène pursed her lips in a full-lipped pout. She could see that Nicolas wanted very much to kiss away her playful sulk, the remedy she desired, but instead, he took her hand in his and drew her down onto the sofa. "It's said the lips are the gateway to the soul, Séro. I never really understood what it meant until I met you. Kissing you is like heaven, only better because I'm not dead yet. It's just..."

Sérolène bit at her bottom lip. She didn't want to talk now. She ached to feel his mouth pressed against hers again, to taste him on her tongue while the river of slow melting fire that made her loins melt, rolled its lazy course through her insides. "Just what, Nico?"

She could see that he knew what she wanted. No man could be more virile ort ardent and she knew he wanted the same thing she did. But he held himself back. And the measure of his restraint showed her that in his heart, love ruled over simple desire.

He gave a long sigh. "I made a promise to your uncle to behave like a perfect gentleman toward you, and when you kiss me the way you do—well, it makes the promise very difficult to keep. I'm allowed to court you now, but I very much doubt your uncle would approve of me kissing you at all. I don't think he'd consider such conduct either proper or gentlemanly."

A part of Sérolène found it noble that Nicolas tried to slow things down. She pushed that part away, and pressed herself up close till the bronze lions of his costume kissed the exposed swell of her bosom. "For you to behave in an ungentlemanly manner, you would have to take liberties where they were unwelcome. A lady has the right to offer her favors, and expect a rightful tribute in reward. Is that not correct?"

Nicolas groaned his assent. Sérolène saw the evidence of his weakening resolution in the rising tent that began to lift his short Greek skirt below the waist. She welcomed it.

"The kisses I give you are favors I bestow with all my heart, Nico. How hurt I would feel if you refused them. The kisses I receive from you are the tribute I expect of one who loves me. How unkind it would be for you to deny me my proper due."

She leaned forward, pressed her mouth on his, forced her tongue past the barrier of his restraint, kissed him and lingered a very long time. His body moved against her, little warning tremors of want, which threatened to erupt into a landslide of desire. She felt no fear. She wanted the great man mountain of his flesh to be moved like that. To quake and tremble at her touch, the way her own body responded to him. She pushed him back and down until she lay atop him, the expanse of his huge body spread out beneath her smaller frame, thigh, to hip, to chest.

"Séro...I beg you."

Her want gave no quarter to his entreaties. She straddled her empire and refused to relinquish it. Her lips clung to his, her torso poured onto his chest as she spilled herself onto him—hands wandering across his shoulders and arms, amazed at the thick layers of muscle. Down they went, toward his thick torso and waist and then lower still, lips still locked together, beyond her control, driven by a basic need to imprint the pattern of his body within the primal tactile memory of her flesh. She grasped his huge haunches, amazed at how they filled her hands; palms sliding up and down on the bare skin of his legs until they found the edge of his short Greek skirt. Lost now, beyond all restraint, she pushed upward toward the hidden source of his manhood.

Bong....bong...bong....bong

The chiming of the mantle clock broke the spell and saved them. Sérolène opened her eyes and sat up. She sat almost astride Nicolas, her long flowing skirts bunched up and disheveled as if she would ride him side saddle. *Dear sweet God, what had she almost done?* Her hands caressed his face in apology and she pressed her lips forward to feast on his sweet mouth in penance. She retreated to the far side of the sofa. Nicolas stood and withdrew to the hearth to collect himself.

Sérolène watched Nicolas as he leaned against the wall like a tiger forced off his prey in mid leap. She marveled at the pillar of a man he'd become. Was that why she had come close to doing the unthinkable? It felt so sweet, and easy, and right. And he had not tried to force her in any way. She had been in control. The decision would have been, and still remained, hers. Another minute with his skin in her hands and she might have lifted his skirt and hers and sent them both to an oblivion of ecstasy…and dishonor. For no matter how much she loved him, they were not yet married, or even betrothed. To make love to him would be a sin, but she felt no shame in the thought. She knew the truth of how she felt. She wanted him, not just his body, but all of him, and she knew he wanted her in the same way. If given the choice between living in disgrace and living respectably without him, she'd have gladly consigned herself to play the fallen flower.

Even now, her thoughts ran confused, fogged by the din of her body. It throbbed, ached, burned with need for him. Her loins oozed desire. She pressed her thighs together to try and ease the want, staring brazenly at Nicolas, wanting him so badly she felt like a bitch in heat, and cared not at all to be so, because who else on earth could claim to be loved, adored, worshipped as she, and that made the wanton ache of desire beautiful and never a reprehensible thing. Her eyes wandered down the length of him, saw the little mountain below the waist of his knee-length armored tunic. She felt passion's ardent, invisible hand slip down her dress to caress and fondle her skin, awakening the full power of her femininity. A soft low moan escaped her throat and she lay her head on the back of the sofa and stared at the gentle pulsing peak below the waist.

Nicolas followed Sérolène's gaze, glancing down at the gentle billowing of his skirt. His face betrayed his mortification. "Séro, I'm sorry, I..."

He turned his body away in an effort to conceal the source of his embarrassment. Sérolène found his modesty unbearably sweet. She smiled and held out her hand to him. He came forward to stand behind the chaise, but didn't trust himself to be able to sit next to her just yet. Sérolène wrapped her hand in his, felt the hard, calloused ridges of his palm against her soft fingers. She kissed Nicolas' palm, pressing her face against his hand.

"There's nothing to be sorry for. My body feels the same way about you as you do about me, Nico, but all these fine layers of cloth succeed in hiding the truth from you. Please don't be embarrassed. I find it rather nice to be so well thought of."

Sérolène looked up at Nicolas with a wide grin. He seemed to see the humor in it all and laughed, which lowered the mountain of his appreciation to a gentle sloping hill. Sérolène beckoned him to join her again on the chaise. Nicolas sat next to her, and she leaned back to recline against his torso, snuggling in the crook of a vast shoulder.

She turned her head to press her nose against his neck, caressing his earlobe and cheek with her fingertips. "I thought of you each day you were away from me, Nico, and dreamt of you each night. The moment right before I went to sleep became the most welcome part of my day, because I always had the pleasure of hoping you would pay me a visit in my dreams."

Nicolas stroked Sérolène's hand. "How I adore you. You please me more than anything in this life, Séro."

Sérolène pulled his face toward her, finding his lips once again with her own. She heard the voice of Julius and then the marquise, followed by the sound of approaching footsteps. Sérolène quickly sat upright, adjusting her gown and coiffure. Nicolas hurried to stand behind the chaise.

A soft knocking echoed against the door frame, and then after a brief pause, the unmasked face of Made de Blaise peered across the threshold into the room. "Come in, Madame. Nicolas and I were just discussing poetry."

Madame de Blaise smiled knowingly as she looked from Nicolas to Sérolène. "Of course you were, my dear. Now put on your masks and come down. The fireworks are about to start. Time for us to join the others."

*

Nicolas donned his helmet and helped Sérolène rise from the chaise. They descended the stairs together as the eighth bell began to toll, making their way into the garden, which teemed with the press of guests vying for the best places to watch the show. Madame de Blaise became separated from them in the throng. Nicolas took Sérolène by the arm, steering her back toward the house to try and escape the press of the crowd and the eager eyes marveling at them, and their costumes. Nicolas spotted an opening in the densely packed mass and led Sérolène toward it, but a man dressed all in black with a flowing cape and a satyr's mask stepped in front of him to block his passage.

The man removed the mask, revealing his face. "You look splendid tonight, Monsieur d'Argentolle. Your costume well suits you."

"Baron de Ginestas," Nicolas said, his senses alert, certain the baron had not appeared by chance.

The baron bowed with deference toward Sérolène, obliging Nicolas to make introductions. "Baron Ginestas, may I present to you Mademoiselle la Vicomtesse de La Bouhaire. Mademoiselle, the Baron de Ginestas," Nicolas said tightly.

Sérolène removed her mask so proper introductions could be made. She seemed to sense the change in Nicolas' mood, however, and stood silent wariness beside him.

"Mademoiselle, would you please forgive me, but the chevalier and I have some personal business which honor requires we tend to at once," the baron said.

Nicolas seethed inwardly at the impertinence of Ginestas in daring to seek him out in his own house. The requirements of honor, however, obligated him to accompany the baron. "My dear *cousine*, I believe I see Madame la Marquise there near the fountain. Would you do me the honor of keeping her company? I promise I shall return to you here in just a short while."

Sérolène's face remained serene but her eyes filled with concern. "As you wish, Nicolas."

The vicomtesse made her way alone toward Madame de Blaise. Both Nicolas and Ginestas bowed to the vicomtesse's retreating back.

The baron grinned toward Nicolas. "Mademoiselle de La Bouhaire is quite a delightful young lady…"

"I forbid you to speak her name to me, do you understand?" Nicolas said with menace, standing almost chest to chest with the baron.

The baron's cheeks flushed with color, but he did not step back. He craned his neck upward to meet the gaze of the much taller chevalier.

"Well, Baron, you've hidden like a rat for the past two days, and now you show yourself in the open on a day when my family is in celebration. I presume your presence here means Mauran's close by and you wish to conclude our business. Well then, so be it. Let's be about this nonsense, and the sooner the better."

The baron bowed his head. "Of course, Monsieur. We have only to speak to Monsieur de Marbéville…"

Nicolas cut off the baron with a scowl. "We will not disrupt my brother for such a farce as this. Lead on Baron. I have promised a lady I will not keep her long in waiting and each moment we delay only prolongs the extent of her inconvenience and mine."

*

Sérolène and Madame de Blaise watched discretely as Nicolas followed Ginestas through the crowd. The men passed behind the fountain, heading for the high hedges at the edge of the garden.

Sérolène's gaze filled with concern. "Where do you think Nicolas could be going, Madame? That man with him, Monsieur de Ginestas, seemed awfully peculiar."

The marquise motioned to one of the house lackeys, who arrived with haste to receive her whispered instructions. After the man hurried off, the marquise turned back toward Sérolène. "I don't know, my dear. Don't you worry, though, I've sent a man to watch over him."

A reveler dressed as an English pirate, sauntered up to the marquise and Sérolène, followed by a similarly dressed companion. The pirate bowed low before Sérolène. His partner performed the same courtesy before the marquise. "Honored Ladies. We beg you grant us the honor of a dance. All night we've admired you and now we beg you most humbly not to refuse us!"

The marquise assented with reluctance. Sérolène followed her lead. As she entered the dance floor, she turned to look for Nicolas, but he had already disappeared into the hedges at the edge of the courtyard.

*

The surgeon paced near the line of trees opposite the rear wall of the old stables, his long face drawn and serious. He wore black from head to toe, except for his stockings, which were white and without a mark or blemish on them. Beneath his black tricorn hat, he wore a heavily powdered wig in the high buckle queue style, a white bow tied around the queue, the top of which dangled just above his shoulders. A few paces behind him, his bag of implements and medicines lay at the foot of a low, stone, wall, which formed the border of the clearing in which the duel he had been asked to monitor would take place.

The old stable buildings stood unused and in disrepair, located on a flat section of the Blaise plantation concealed from the view of the château. The partial concealment of the site made it ideal for dueling—a pastime by nature both private and secretive. The rectangular area had been marked at regular intervals with torches staked in the ground to provide appropriate light. At the center, Montbatre, acting as a second, engaged with Mauran in a practice bout, warming up the Vidame de Saint-Dié, for the pending encounter.

Montbatre and Mauran had been exercising for some time as they waited for Nicolas to appear. The surgeon looked on, impressed by Mauran's skill. He had no doubt the Vidame de Saint-Dié would be more than a match for most. The doctor knew nothing of the skill of the man who had yet to arrive, not that it mattered. He had seen many duels in his time and hoped both men would live to see the sunrise, but one never knew with affairs of honor. Besides he had been well paid to render his discretion and his services for the affair.

The surgeon glanced up at the sound of approaching footsteps, halting in his steps as he saw the curious combination of the Baron de Ginestas in his all-black costume, satyr's mask and flowing cape, escorting the presumed chevalier, dressed in a fantastic costume in the manner of Alexander the Great. As soon as the two entered the rectangular area, Mauran retreated to the far side of the clearing in company with Montbatre. Ginestas introduced Nicolas to the surgeon. Nicolas bowed, and declared his readiness to begin at once.

The surgeon frowned. It seemed most irregular to start things without the required seconds on the field and the chevalier had brought no men to attend him. The surgeon looked to Ginestas to gauge his reaction, but the baron said nothing.

"The Comte de Marbéville has not yet arrived, Messieurs. We cannot begin until all members of both parties are here," the surgeon said.

Nicolas shook his head. "My brother has better things to do than occupy himself with such foolishness as this. The fête tonight is for him, and I will not have him disturbed. The Vidame de Saint-Dié is here, I am here. No more is required for us to settle matters."

"I could stand for the chevalier," Ginestas offered.

Nicolas shook his head again. "Thank you, Baron, but in that case, I prefer to engage without a second."

The surgeon saw how things stood between the baron and the chevalier, and guessed the sentiments between the principals likely to be no better and perhaps even worse. "I suppose I could stand in place of Monsieur de Marbéville. If it should be acceptable to the chevalier."

"Do as you like," Nicolas said tersely.

*

Ginestas nodded his assent to the surgeon's offer, eager for any excuse to begin the business at hand. He motioned for his valet to fetch the weapons to be used. "Splendid. Now we can begin."

The lackey brought forth a long wooden box holding two identical swords, offering Nicolas, as the challenged party, the first choice of weapons.

Nicolas yielded the advantage to his opponent. "Let Mauran have his preference."

Ginestas nodded out of courtesy. "That is most gallant of you, Monsieur."

Ginestas heart raced as he admired Nicolas' well-muscled form, much of it amply revealed by his short Greek tunic. *So they were right about your honorable nature. More's the pity, my beau young Adonis.*

The lackey opened the weapons case for Mauran, who selected the uppermost blade. Montbatre glared at Mauran. "That sword seems unlucky. Best to take the other."

The vidame accepted his second's advice and returned the blade he had chosen to its case. He selected the lower weapon, hefting it for weight and feel. "Yes, this one will do nicely."

Mauran reached out to touch the rapier to test its sharpness. Montbatre caught him sharply by the wrist, steering the vidame's hand away from the exposed blade with a firm grasp. "I wouldn't do that if I were you. It is very sharp, and you might injure yourself."

Mauran looked as though he might protest, but Montbatre maintained his warning gaze. Ginestas watched in silence as the wheels of comprehension turned slowly in the dupe's head. The light of awareness broke across Mauran's eyes. The vidame looked back at him as if he wanted to laugh. Poisoning a dueling blade was a dastardly and ignoble thing to do, but as expected, Mauran made no protest. Rather his eyes seemed to shout, *how marvelous for me!*

*

Nicolas took the remaining blade and hefted it for feel. He removed his red cloak and the short Greek sword strapped to his waist, to prepare for the pending combat. As the surgeon took his things, Nicolas heard a noise behind him and looked up to see a crowd of boys perched on the roof of the old stable to observe the forbidden spectacle of mortal combat. Along the edge of the shoulder-high stone wall, which ran along the back of the building, the heads of several coach drivers and attendants could also be seen. *They must have followed us as we left the château.* His own valet Julius stood among the crowd of onlookers. Nicolas beckoned him forward. Julius hurried to his master's side, trotting through a dense cloud of moths and other nocturnal insects buzzing over the field of combat, attracted by the light from the torches.

"Julius, what are you doing out here? Why aren't you at the château?"

"Madame sent me to follow you, Monseigneur. She and the vicomtesse were worried," Julius explained.

"I might have guessed. Take my things will you."

Julius gathered his master's Greek sword, helmet, and cloak and moved to stand behind his master near the tree line. Ginestas walked to the center of the rectangle, ready to begin the ritual of the duel. Both combatants moved to take their places at opposite ends of the rectangle, their seconds beside them. While Nicolas remained still, his sword at his side, Mauran strutted about with confidence, swinging his sword back and forth with bravado. Nicolas watched his opponent with care. *He wasn't so sanguine when I first arrived. I wonder what's happened to change things.*

Ginestas looked from one combatant to the other. "Are both parties determined their differences can only be resolved through honorable combat?"

Mauran spoke to Montbatre, who as second, turned to reply on his behalf, as the ritual of honor required.

"Monsieur de Mauran's honor can only be satisfied by the shedding of blood."

Nicolas turned to the surgeon, who acted as his second. "He is a fool, but I shall oblige him with the blood he seeks, though it shall not be my own."

"The chevalier is also so resolved," the surgeon said.

Nicolas studied Mauran as the last steps of the prelude to combat came to a close. The bugs flitting around the light of the torches seemed oddly attracted to Mauran's naked blade, as if it were a large metal flower. His own blade drew no such attention. *How very odd.*

Ginestas raised a hand high above him. "Both gentlemen will approach and salute each other."

The seconds retreated to stand behind Ginestas as the combatants moved to the ready position. Mauran swaggered forward, his confidence growing with every step he took.

You'll lose that absurd grin soon enough, Nicolas resolved, irritated by his opponent's uncalled for conceit. *Wait*, his intuition warned. *There's something you've missed.* No man behaved in such a cavalier manner when faced with death by the sword, not even experienced swordsmen. *There is something wrong here. Stop looking only with your eyes. Remember what Vesterkamp taught you. Use your perception to see the truth.*

Both men moved to the proper distance, just paces away from each other. Nicolas breathed slowly in an effort to calm his mind and allow it to perceive what his eyes had missed. He took in the entire scene around him, trying to feel, scent, touch the thing amiss, as he searched for the clues he needed to unlock the puzzle of Mauran's behavior.

Mauran still looked smug and confident. So did Ginestas…and even Montbatre. *They know something you don't know.* Nicolas realized. *They are all in on it! How can that be?*

Nicolas and Mauran saluted each other, bringing their blades toward their chests. A large white moth circled about Mauran's blade and landed near the point. It stayed on its perch not more than a few seconds before dropping to the ground, stone dead. Nicolas understood at last. *Poisoned! The blade's been poisoned*!

*

"En garde!" Ginestas shouted, lowering his hand to signal the start of the combat.

Mauran ran forward at once, thrusting eagerly in an attempt to land any touch he could, the furious savagery of his attack driving Nicolas back as he struggled to avoid the likely fatal contact of his opponent's blade. Nicolas parried every attack, absorbing his opponent's energy but not launching a counter of his own. *Why would Mauran do such a thing? We have no real quarrel between us. He chose to flee our encounter and dishonor himself. Who has put him up to this vile and dishonorable act?*

Incensed by the idea of the double game being played, Nicolas went on the offensive as Mauran began to tire, the impetus of the vidame's energy wastefully spent in the violence of his initial attacks. Nicolas surged forward, pressing his opponent on all sides. He swung the rapier in wide oblique arcs to force his opponent to cover his flanks. Mauran stumbled backward, Nicolas maneuvered him toward the corner of the rectangle where Montbatre stood, cutting off the angles of escape. *I've only one shot at this. I must get everything just right.*

Nicolas cut heavily from above, riding the expected parry from Mauran into a clinch, then forcing his opponent back toward his own second with a push. As Mauran retreated, Nicolas aimed an overhead cut at the center of Mauran's forehead. The blade whistled down in a blur. Desperate to avoid the blow, Mauran raised his sword horizontally to deflect it. Nicolas came down on the center of the blade, the force of his blow driving Mauran's point downward at an angle so the poisoned tip passed dangerously close to Nicolas' chest. Mauran thrust forward with all his strength, intent upon running Nicolas through.

As Mauran lunged, Nicolas flicked his wrist counter clockwise, using the force of his opponent's lunge for leverage as he spun the blade, twisting the tip up and back. For a split second, the poisoned rapier floated mid-air with the point turned backward toward Montbatre as it came out of Mauran's hand. Nicolas surged forward, thrusting his own blade through Mauran's heart with his right hand, while with his left he pushed the hilt of Mauran's reversed blade toward Montbatre. The weapon pierced the startled second in the side. There were gasps as both men fell to the ground. Everything happened so quickly, no one seemed quite sure what had occurred in the torch-lit darkness.

Nicolas knew with certainty he had killed Mauran. He looked instead toward the fallen Montbatre. *If I am right about your vile treachery, then you will soon be dead too, though the wound I gave you would not normally be fatal. If I am wrong, then you have nothing to fear, save the ridicule of being injured in another's duel. Perhaps you have acted honorably, in which case you have nothing greater than your embarrassment to regret. If not, then you deserve the death coming to you.*

Nicolas bowed and returned to his starting position. "My honor has been satisfied."

The surgeon hurried to Nicolas' side. They both bowed once more in unison as the ritual of honor required. Nicolas eyed the baron coldly as he spoke to the surgeon. "You may return to your primary duties, Monsieur, though only Montbatre has need of your services now."

Ginestas stood in a state of utter bewilderment, his plans suddenly thrown into disarray. The chevalier knew by looking at Ginestas that he served as someone's hired assassin. Had not his father warned him that their enemies would try and strike? Now he had to discover who had paid the scoundrel's black wages. *Ginestas is the key, and he had Montbatre in league with him, I am sure. Perhaps I am not the only target, or even the principal one. Father warned of trouble before we reached France. I sense this is the beginning of it.*

Nicolas approached the baron, motioning for his valet to bring him his cloak, sword, and helmet. "You will leave our lands at once, and I do not wish to see you here ever again. Hover too near my torch, baron, and perhaps next time, the flames of reckoning will consume you, as well."

Nicolas then turned his back on Ginestas and began the walk back toward the château. His valet came alongside him, matching his steps.

"Come, Julius, I promised the vicomtesse I'd return to her shortly, and already I've been much longer than I intended. Give Madame de Blaise what excuses you will for my absence, but I forbid you to say anything of what you just witnessed."

"Yes, Monseigneur."

Julius helped Nicolas refit his costume. Nicolas saw his valet's hands trembling as he worked, his thoughts perhaps still preoccupied with the carnage he had just witnessed. Julius peered over his shoulder toward the members of the dueling party. Nicolas paid them no attention at all.

*

Back at the center of the clearing, the Baron de Ginestas stood several paces back from the prone figures of Mauran and Montbatre. The cloak draped over Mauran's body by the surgeon, told Ginestas all he needed to know of the vidame's fate. The surgeon knelt beside Montbatre, who had pulled Mauran's blade from his side.

Ginestas summoned his lackey to his side. The man hurried forward. "Collect both weapons, then have them melted down at once, do you hear? Be careful you do not touch the blade with your hands."

Ginestas turned his gaze to Montbatre. Their eyes met. He saw disbelief and despondency in Montbatre's gaze. The surgeon moved away to retrieve some fresh dressings from his case. Montbatre went to kneel at his friend's side. Montbatre pulled at his sleeve.

"Listen to me, Baron. He's a real devil, he is. He guessed our secret, I'm sure of it. This wound he gave me is no accident. The bastard's killed me for certain, though I'm still not sure how he managed it."

Serves you right for picking that bungler Mauran for the task. Ah well, at least he is dead too. The baron removed a small vial of clear liquid from his pocket. "Rest easily, brave Montbatre, and drink this antidote. It's bitter, but it will make you well in no time."

The baron saw both hope and desperation in Montbatre's gaze. "There is an antidote? You did not tell me. I must have it at once!"

Montbatre took the vial and swallowed the contents in one gulp. His eyes widened in horror, but before he could draw a single breath in protest, his heart had already stopped beating. Ginestas picked up the open vial with his handkerchief and returned it to his pocket. He reached inside his waistcoat to retrieve a small paring knife, then bent over Montbatre, as if saying a prayer. He stuck the knife into the wound, widening it so more blood poured forth. Satisfied no one would suspect any other reason as the cause of death, he returned the knife to his pocket. As he heard the surgeon returning with fresh bandages he began to weep most piteously.

"There's no need for undue worry, Monsieur. There is much blood, but no vitals have been struck," the surgeon reassured him.

"He is dead!" Ginestas wailed. "See for yourself. The blade must have penetrated enough to sever a blood vessel. Just look at how he bleeds. Oh my poor friend Montbatre."

Ginestas carried on for some time, to make sure his protestations appeared earnest and his explanation had been believed. The surgeon seemed perplexed. He stood over the corpse, no doubt wondering how he'd gotten things so wrong. He seemed about to kneel and take another look at the source of the injury, when the baron laid a hand on his arm. The baron's opposite hand held a heavy purse.

"I don't blame you, Monsieur. You've done your duty to the utmost. I shall see you are well rewarded for your discretion and your services. Best to leave things now as they are."

The surgeon seemed to weigh the value of the gold against the profit in questioning the cause of death. In the end, he accepted the purse and with it the baron's explanation, as Ginestas had expected.

The surgeon shook his head ruefully. "Poor Montbatre, how unlucky to be killed in another's duel. I'll get them both in the carriage, Baron, if you don't mind your man lending me a hand. Leave it to me to take care of the documents and such."

Ginestas nodded, content the cleanup would at least be handled according to plan. He reflected on the duel and the chevalier's skill with admiration. *First touch to you, my handsome young Achilles. How like that fabled warrior you are, in beauty and in terrible might. Yet, Achilles had a fatal weakness and I will wager so do you, and what a pretty little heel she is. We shall meet again soon enough, my beau chevalier, and then we shall see whose flame burns the hottest and the longest.*

*

"Nicolas! There you are at last. Madame de Blaise and I were both very worried about what you'd gotten up to with your mysterious companion."

The man with whom Sérolène danced seemed about to protest at being left on the floor in such haste until he saw his rival was Alexander the Great. He good-naturedly relinquished the vicomtesse, doffed his hat to history's greatest captain, and went off in search of another partner.

Nicolas smiled down at Sérolène. "I see you've kept yourself merry enough in my absence. Where has Maman gone? I hope this isn't her idea of playing a proper chaperone to you. Did my mother not understand she was to keep you out of the grasp of everyone but me?"

Sérolène removed her mask and scrunched up her nose at Nicolas. "You must not blame Madame, Nicolas, the fault is entirely yours. You chose to abandon me for the company of that horrible little man, did you not?"

Nicolas acknowledged the fairness of Sérolène's judgment with a grin, desperate to kiss the scolding pout from her face as part of his penance.

Sérolène noted the particular way he looked at her. "What is it, Nico?"

A fanfare of trumpets and the press of the crowd interrupted any answer.

"Ladies, gentlemen, distinguished guests, please move forward toward the western part of the courtyard. The fireworks are about to begin!"

Nicolas offered Sérolène his arm. "Come with me."

*

While the crowd pressed forward to gain the best viewing positions for the display, Nicolas led Sérolène through the garden. They made their way by a hidden path to a small clearing near the border of the cane fields. There, they at last found both privacy and space. As the fireworks began, drawing the attention of everyone, Nicolas found a comfortable place at the base of an old oak, where they could sit and enjoy the display unseen and undisturbed.

Sérolène sat across Nicolas' lap to avoid soiling her dress. She draped her right arm around Nicolas' shoulder, leaving her left hand free to point with delight at the bursting fireworks overhead. Her excited cries of observation provided a counterpoint to the general noise of the spectacle.

"Did you see it, Nico? A shooting star!"

Nicolas looked up, admiring the faint trail of stardust as it flashed across the sky. Sérolène grasped Nicolas' hand and held it between both of hers. "Quick, make a wish."

Sérolène paused for a moment, and then looked at Nicolas. "What did you wish for, Nico?"

Nicolas grinned. "I thought if you told your wishes, they wouldn't come true."

Sérolène rolled her eyes, determined to persuade Nicolas to divulge his secret. "That's only for birthday wishes. It doesn't apply to shooting stars…or wishes you share with those you love."

Nicolas chuckled. "Oh? I think, Mademoiselle, you're making that up entirely."

Sérolène stroked Nicolas' cheek above the dimple, caressing his earlobe with the tip of her fingers. "Perhaps you are right, Monsieur, but nevertheless I quite demand to know."

Nicolas pressed his lips against the back of Sérolène's hand, pausing to admire the long delicate taper of her fingers. "Well, I suppose there's no harm in telling you. I wished for a life filled with an eternity of your kisses."

Sérolène laid her head against the impossible bulk of Nicolas' finely chiseled sword arm. She purred with love and contentment, pressed her lips against the side of Nicolas' arm, then raised her head to kiss him on the side of the neck. "There, that's one."

She planted another kiss on his cheek. "And two."

Nicolas gave Sérolène a teasing grin. "That's a good start, Séro. But you've still quite a long way to go before reaching eternity."

Sérolène turned to face hm. Nicolas' eyes reflected the light from the nearby torches and the bursting fireworks above. "Then, Monsieur, you'd best live up to your reputation...and have the boldness to make your wish come true."

Nicolas took Sérolène's face in his hands. His lips covered hers, which parted eagerly in surrender. Fireworks burst above them, the brilliant flashes ignored and unseen, as underneath the canopy of real and artificial stars, they began in earnest, their quest for eternity.

APPENDIX

Principal Characters

House of Montferraud

Nicolas Étienne Alexandre Hyacinthe-Christophe de Montferraud d'Argentolle - (Chevalier and Vicomte d'Argentolle)

Édouard Charles Pierre Marie François de Montferraud de Blaise - (Chevalier de Perinne, Marquis de Blaise)

Francis Christophe Alexandre Honoré de Montferraud de Marbéville - (Chevalier and Comte de Marbéville)

Ouragon Galtung van Hardanger de Montferraud de Blaise - (Marquise de Blaise)

Sérolène Adélaïde Isabelle de Saint-Giresse de La Bouhaire - (Vicomtesse de La Bouhaire)

Guy Christian Hervé Rocheforte de Salvagnac - (Baron de Salvagnac)

Agnès Caroline Marie de Saint-Giresse de Salvagnac - (Baronne de Salvagnac)

Julienne Claire Sophie Rocheforte de Salvagnac - (Comtesse de Marbéville)

Éléonore Louisa Charlotte Rocheforte de Salvagnac

Others of note

Charlotte Marie du Plessis de Talonge - (Comtesse de Talonge)

Madame Tarnaut - Governess to the Vicomtesse de La Bouhaire

---

[i] The Collection of the Kyoto Costume Institute. Fashion. A history from the 18th to the 20th Century. Pg. 72. Customers selected the embroidered fabric, which was then measured and tailored to suit. For some excellent visual examples of male and female styles of the time, see: The Collection of the Kyoto Costume Institute. Fashion. A history from the 18th to the 20th Century. Pages 25-117.

[ii] Sample dishes from a royal meal served for Marie Antoinette quoted in L'Almanach des Gourmands pour 1862, by Charles Monselet. Her Majesty's Dinner, Thursday 24 July 1788 at Trianon.

[iii] 18th Century Hair & Wig Styling. History and step-by-step techniques. Kendra Van Cleave. ISBN 978-0-692-22043-6. www.18thCenturyHair.com. See pages 276-279 for examples of this style. I highly recommend this book for anyone interested in hairstyles of the time and how they were created.

[iv] A female dog. Vulgar slang for bitch

[v] About $2,500,000

[vi] The most distinguished rank of nobility

[vii] A well-known women's prison of the time in Paris.

[viii] About $5,000,000

[ix] http://en.wikipedia.org/wiki/French_Navy One does not prepend mon to the name of the rank when addressing an officer in the French Navy (that is, not mon capitaine, but simply capitaine)

[x] See 18th Century Hair & Wig Styling, pg. 211, for an example of this style, which resembles a a large upside down pear in shape, with curls and adornments attached. This style typically stood sixteen inches or more above the wearer's scalp. .

[xi] For my dearest love. The breath of my life, the pulse of my heart, the light of my soul. Forever and always.

Made in the USA
San Bernardino, CA
22 November 2017